SCHISM

CHAPTER 1

WEST LONDON, APRIL 2016

David hurried out of the shop and started to thread his way through the evening streets. Despite the milder weather arriving from the south, the evenings still retained their chill of the receding winter months. David wore his knitted gloves. Under his arm he was clutching a rectangular package, wrapped in plain brown paper and secured with triple-twist twine. In the pit of his stomach, an unfamiliar feeling of apprehension gnawed away at him.

Using the scant light emitted from the window of the old antiques shop, David checked his watch, the hands read; 22:01. "Damn it! Stopped." Not that it mattered. Time was not his friend tonight and although he didn't know it yet, time was running out for David. In fact, the instant he had handed over his cash to the esoteric shopkeeper, David had entered into a transaction he could not possibly afford. Equally, he had no way of predicting the dire consequences his purchase would bring about, not just for him, but for the entire planet. It all started with the innocuous, rectangular package wrapped in brown paper and secured with triple-twist twine currently nestling under David's arm. He continued his journey, taking the most direct route back to his home, now and again stopping and checking over his shoulder to ensure he wasn't being observed.

Twenty minutes later David was back among the meagre surroundings of his bedroom. He had managed to slip through the front door without alerting his landlady; Mrs Reynolds, the ever-present sentinel. Mrs Reynolds was an imposing third generation German Jew, whose family had managed to escape the tyranny of the NAZI uprising back in 1938. After surviving the bombings of Goering's Luftwaffe attacks, they settled in the South East of England. She had married a respectable Jewish business owner and enjoyed a comfortable life, but twelve years later he died and she was left with his debts. Mr Reynolds had managed to keep a secret gambling addiction from his wife and when he gambled his business away to the horses, he took his own life rather than live with the shame he'd brought to the family. More than a decade later and with no income of her own, the bills kept on coming. Mrs Reynolds had been forced to rent out the top room of her house so she could afford the mortgage. David was two weeks behind on his rent.

David quietly closed the door to his bedroom and ensured that it was locked. In the two steps it took for him to cover the distance to his bed, he heard the familiar groan of the floorboards outside his room.

"Oh, nosey old biddy." He thought, as he gently placed the parcel on the end of his bed and shrugged the coat off his shoulders. He let the coat fall to the floor, where it joined the rest of his wardrobe and started to attack the string with bitten-down fingernails. From the corner of his eye, he noticed two foot-shaped shadows move in the light that was streaming underneath his door.

"Good evening. Mrs Reynolds." He shouted through the closed door. "Sorry if I disturbed you. I'll pay you some rent tomorrow." He lied. The shadows shuffled away, the gentle creak announcing the silent departure of his duenna.

David counted to ten in his head, before cracking open his door enough to see down the landing. He was just in time to see the departing shadow of a lumpish figure as it disappeared from sight, a slight wheezing accompanying it as it receded from view. Satisfied that he wouldn't be disturbed again, David returned his attention to the parcel which was still perched at the foot of his bed. He picked it up, and reassured by its weight, he started to tug at the knotted string again. This time he tried using his teeth to loosen the binds that the shopkeeper had used.

"Christ! That freaky old man was determined to make sure this damned thing was tied up nice and tight." David said out loud to himself in frustration. "It's almost as if he didn't want me to be able to open it."

He thought about the bizarre conversation he'd had with the elderly shopkeeper, whilst browsing the curious collection of artefacts displayed in the dusty shop. He remembered the old man had a funny accent, although he couldn't place where it was from exactly. Eastern European, Dutch perhaps? What he did know was that the shopkeeper was old...very old. David's stepfather would have said; *"That man's so old he knew God when he were a lad."* Out of all the relics littering the shelves of the shop, the strange old man was very keen for David to see one item in particular. Perhaps a little too keen, now David came to think about it. At first, David had rejected the notion that he needed to purchase a plain box with no obvious function. Pretty though it was. His memory phased in and out with pieces of the conversation.

"But this box is no ordinary box, young man." The shopkeeper had insisted. "If you want to make a serious amount of money, all you need is this box, David." The shopkeeper had grabbed hold of David's hand and cupped it with an icy palm, pressing hard and drawing him in closer. David could smell the garlic and brandy on the man's breath. He recalled the old man fixing him with a long, poignant stare before continuing. "Why don't you take it home and try it out? If you still don't want it by this time tomorrow you can bring it back and I will give you a full refund. Do not make the mistake of turning your back on destiny, David."

It transpired that at this exact moment in David's life, motivation by the potential of making money was all the encouragement he needed. So, here he was now fighting to unwrap the package and getting more irate as the knots only seemed to tighten the harder he pulled at them.

One of the knots began to loosen, just enough for David to prize the twine over the edge. Now divested of the triple-twist, he sought out the folded edge of the paper with his index finger and inserted it under the gap. In one swift movement, David swiped his finger through the adhesive tape that the shopkeeper had used to secure the ends. The fresh tape had not had enough time to bond with the paper and easily detached itself without much resistance. David carefully slid the paper wrapping down with one hand while gripping the edge of the package with the other, revealing with almost reverential care the treasured contents within.

He let the discarded wrapping fall to the floor and paid no more mind to it. David's attention was now fully focused upon the object he was holding in his hands. For a long time he just stood, unmoving in the middle of his room, staring at his purchase while being bathed in the scintillating moonlight that penetrated through his window. Shafts of lunar illumination played across his face, casting their sinister shadows over the contours of his features.

The rectangular shape that had demanded so much attention was roughly the same shape as a monopoly game board. The base was constructed from a grey metallic substance, that seemed to shimmer without any light shining on it. The sides felt like they were made from a smooth glass, which reflected the shimmering light from the base up towards the top panel, which was silky-smooth to the touch and completely opaque. There were no visible joins or discernible markings evident. The entire box appeared to be a single construct devoid of any decoration or design.

David could see his reflection staring back at him from the highly polished milk-glass surface and realised his mouth was hanging open. It was a characteristic not peculiar to David alone, but one which his mother would usually be on hand to chide him over... "You'll catch flies if you go around with your mouth open, Davy." She would say. However, today she was not available to issue such a rebuke. In fact, David hadn't seen much of his mother since he left home for Uni, and that was coming up to eighteen months ago. Despite the difficulties he was having with the budgeting of his meagre salary, he was determined to live his life independently from his mother's influence. He knew she would not be able to help him out financially, she could barely make ends meet for herself. No, it was clear to David that he was going to have to learn to support himself and the box was going to be his means to achieve this. He pushed all other thoughts from his mind and returned his attention to the object in his hands.

Over the next half hour, he studied the box with forensic care. He angled his desk lamp trying to get better light. The box seemed to absorb the entire 40 watts of energy his bulb was capable of emitting. He opened his desk drawer and rummaged about in the accumulated collection of detritus. In amongst the dead batteries, old charging cables and leaking Biros, he found the unopened SuperBrite LED torch he'd been given for his last birthday. 'The Power of the Sun in Your Hands,' the catchy slogan read on the packaging. He ripped open the blister-pack with his teeth and removed the torch. He pressed the rubber switch located in the base and squinted as the clinical brightness of the diodes bathed his room in crisp, white light. He directed the beam onto the surface of the box. His room went dark as the box absorbed every last lumen. The aluminium body of the torch heated up as the box drained the power from the batteries in ten seconds flat. David yelped and dropped the torch, which fused into the melted fibres of his polyester carpet.

"Bugger!"

He picked the box up and started to turn it over. As soon as his bare hands came into contact with the strange material, he realised it was warm to the touch. Something he hadn't noticed before because of his gloves. There was an tangible feeling of warmth radiating from it. The air immediately surrounding it was unaffected. But without physically being warm the box was warm. He placed his palms on the top and felt a slight surge in heat. He quickly withdrew his hands, frightened he'd get burned again. The box reacted to his touch. The surface changed slightly revealing two shapes. The moment David withdrew his hands the shapes disappeared in a ripple and the surface smoothed out again leaving the top in its pristine condition. David reached out a tentative hand again, this time leaving it on the surface a bit longer. He felt the heat build again, but it didn't burn. He placed the other hand on the surface of the box and watched as two hand-shaped indentations materialised, each with hundreds of tiny perforations covering their surface. He removed his hands and the indentations disappeared again, replaced with the unblemished glossy surface. This discovery warranted a single utterance.

"Cool."

As far as David could see, there was nothing else about the box that gave any indication as to its purpose, with the exception of the magic hand prints, which invited you to place your hands into them without directly telling you to do so.

He walked over to the small table in the corner of his room, sweeping the contents away using his forearm and sending them crashing to the floor. The noise was bound to alert Mrs Reynolds, but David was too enamoured by the box to care. He lowered the box onto the table using the same amount of care a first-time mother would placing her new born baby in its crib. He hooked an ankle around a nearby stool and dragged it across the carpeted floor and sat down, his back ramrod straight, his head unbowed, eyes looking straight ahead but not seeming to see anything. Now that he was touching it, David was transfixed by its spell. This was one example of the strange allure that the box possessed. It had an almost mesmeric attraction which effused over one's consciousness, as if something 'otherworldly' was in control. Subconsciously, however it guided the operator instinctively, which was just as well as there were no instructions that came with it. The box built a growing desire with the rewarding feeling of sublime satisfaction once you had completely surrendered your will to it, and that was exactly what David did.

Using the tips of his fingers, David began feeling around the edges and side of the box until he came across a slight indentation. He pushed it and felt a small square give way to the pressure of his touch. A soft click announced the sudden detachment of a hidden section which now ejected itself, much like a CD ROM tray would on a laptop computer. David grabbed hold of the object and pulled it clear. He inspected this new addition to the box, noticing that it was an Isosceles triangle, roughly three inches by six. Offset at the top centre was a transparent circular disc made from a crystal and fashioned into a lens. David placed a finger behind the lens and noticed that it had magnified to twice its original size. He set the triangle down in the centre of the opaline surface, where it seemed to almost levitate on a micro-cushion of air the way two opposite poles of a magnet would repel each other. The slightest touch, the merest breath, would be enough to send the device skidding across the frictionless surface. For now, it just sat suspended in mid-air defying gravity.

David instinctively glanced over his shoulder checking for any lurking shadows. He lifted both of his hands and simultaneously placed them, palm-down onto the box and watched the two identical indentations appear again. This time though, there was a palpable shift in the mood of the room. Something vaguely sinister pervaded the atmosphere as the box appeared to be breathing. It began to emit an invisible wave of pulsating dark energy. The instant David's hands touched the surface, two steel bands sprung over his wrists accompanied by a metallic swishing noise, locking his hands to the box. The steel bands completed their arc and disappeared into the surface where unseen mechanisms grabbed hold of them, drawing them down and tight over David's hands. At the same time pushing up through the myriad of perforations, hundreds of hollow pointed needles drove upwards, embedding their razor-sharp tips into the fleshy underside of David's trapped hands. Oddly there was no sensation of pain, neither was there any suggestion of panic on David's face. He calmly accepted what the box was doing to him, as if it was the most natural thing in the world to be happening to him right now.

Within seconds of the needles plunging into David's skin, the surface of the box began to change. Beneath the laminations five rivulets of red, semi-viscous liquid emanated from each hand branching off from the fingertips and began to travel along hidden channels. From the left-hand side, they rose up the edge of the surface before arcing over to the right, where they started to reveal a row of numerical digits ranging from zero to nine. The right-hand threads fed across the bottom to the far left, the advancing red ink describing all twenty-six letters of the alphabet in a Germanic gothic script.

Finally, both rivulets joined up in the centre to complete the outline of a magnificent eagle, its pointed wings outstretched and its hook-beaked face pointing to the left. As the red outlines filtered downwards, the most chilling finale was etched. In its taloned feet, the eagle clutched an oak leaf circle surrounding and instantly recognised icon of hatred…a Fylfot. Better known to millions of persecuted souls as the NAZI Swastika. Two words resolved at either end of the wing tips. 'JA' and 'NEIN'.

The box was now complete in David's blood and was intrinsically linked to his own life-force. During the solitary initiation ceremony, it had bonded with his molecules at a para-physiological level.

The needles automatically retracted and the steel bands were released with a clunk. He watched as they swished back with the same alarming speed they had emerged with. David removed his hands from the box and brought them up to his face for closer inspection. Small red dots covered the entire underside of his palms. Ripples ricocheted around the top of the box for a few seconds before solidifying once again into the smooth opalesque surface. A slight numbing sensation began to build from the centre of David's body. He looked down at the box and saw the intricate gothic design comprising of the letters and numbers. The chilling NAZI eagle drawn in his own blood and the hovering planchette.

"That was trippy." He managed to croak. Seconds later his world dissolved into the inky blackness of oblivion as David passed out.

CHAPTER 2

PROPAGANDA MINISTRY

WILHELM STRASSE, BERLIN

APRIL 1943

A solitary black telephone sat on an empty leather-topped desk in an airless room, ringing to itself. The only source of natural light was provided by a skylight window high up in the vaulted ceiling. It struggled to give out more than a few candles-worth of light. The shrill chimes of the ringing bell reverberated off the stark brick walls. With the exception of the desk, the room was utterly devoid of furniture. The telephone continued to ring impatiently.

Strewn across the faded linoleum, sheets of paper were left where they had fallen. Documents bearing the official seal of Herr Goebbels office littered the floor. A jack boot left a muddy print on one of the sheets of paper stamped: 'Project Zeitsprung.'

The office showed signs of being vacated in a hurry. Anyone looking closely through the murky gloom would have noticed the deep gouges in the lino, denoting heavy furniture being dragged over it. The edges of the door frame had been splintered and chipped, evidence of cumbersome filing cabinets filled with highly classified documents, carelessly being dragged through by the clean-up squad in their haste to evacuate the room. Sitting in the centre of the room was a wire wastepaper basket. A halo of cold grey ash had spilled over the rim, indicating the charred remains of the incinerated documents were not intended for unauthorised eyes. The office, stripped bare of its erstwhile importance now stood empty. The only item left behind was the wooden desk, on top of which sang the ringing black telephone. It rang and rang and rang.

From outside the abandoned office came the distant sound of urgent footsteps echoing down a long corridor, they grew louder. They abruptly halted outside the heavy wood panelled door and a jangling of keys scraped the brass lock plate. The door burst open revealing a tall man dressed in an immaculately pressed field-grey uniform of an SS Schutzstaffel officer. He stepped into the room and looked around, identifying where the source of the noise was coming from. He spotted the telephone and strode across the office to reach it, his polished boots clicking against the hard surface of the floor. He stretched out a single gloved hand and abruptly silenced the ringing by snatching up the receiver.

"Allo." he barked into the Bakelite. "Was ist es?" He listened briefly to the voice at the other end of the line and immediately stiffened.

"You are positive?" A slight tone of unease was detectable in his voice. He bought his thumb and forefinger up and pinched the bridge of his nose, screwing his eyes shut for a brief moment before issuing his reply

"Very well. Have your team put on standby and alert von Riker's office. I will call Obergruppenführer Glock and arrange transport at once, expect to receive us tomorrow morning, Auf Wiedersehen."

He paused for a significant moment, staring blankly into the gloom of the empty office. Still holding onto the receiver, he tapped the cradle with his fingers a couple of times and waited for the operator. After a moment, a voice came on the line. He spoke quickly.

"Allo, this is Sturmbannführer Schaffer. Connect me to General Glock's office at once."

He needn't say anything else; the operator knew exactly who General Glock was and where to reach him day or night.

Obergruppenführer Claus Glock, to give him his full rank and title, was renowned throughout the German army.

Originally an early SA member, Claus Glock was involved at the very beginning of the SS's rise to power. He played a central part in the violence that erupted in the Munich Bürgerbräukeller. After sixteen NAZI party members and four policemen were killed in the failed beer-hall putsch, he fled the Weimar Republic and sheltered in the Austrian countryside, along with Joseph Berchtold and a few other early leadership figures. The authorities caught up with him two days later and he was brought to trial at the People's Court, where he pleaded guilty to the charge of civil disobedience. The court awarded him a fine of 500 Marks and placed a minor reprimand on his record. The lenient and some say bias judges clearing Glock of any major involvement.

During the 'Night of the Long Knives', Glock saw an opportunity to raise his status within the NAZI party and was instrumental in the murder of several high-ranking leadership members of the SA. It was Glock who pulled the trigger in the cold-blooded shooting of Ernst Röhm, as he sat in his Stadelheim prison cell.

He was involved in the Kristallnacht Pogrom, where he commanded a brigade of Himmler's SS thugs to drive out Jewish businesses. Homes, hospitals, synagogues and schools were ransacked as attackers demolished buildings with sledgehammers leaving splintered glass strewn across the streets of Germany.

By the spring of 1940 he once again came to the notice of senior commanders for his ruthless efficiency as he led the successful invasion of the low countries and with it, Germany's unstoppable drive into France. The paramilitary party became the Waffen SS, and Major Glock was promoted to the rank of General and given the SS title; Obergruppenführer, second only in seniority to the Reichsmashall. His reputation permeated through the ranks right up to the highest echelons. From spud peeling privates to Field Marshals, by the summer of 1941, everyone in the German army had heard the name Claus Glock.

By September of the same year, Himmler arranged for Glock to be recalled from frontline duties and he was given command of the PSD, the SS Paranormal Division. No better man could have been hand selected for this job.

As with most of the members of the SS, Glock was a fastidious pedant. He was a diminutive and angular man allegedly in his late 40s, but looked somewhere north of his 60s. He had a sallow complexion which gave the impression of him already being half-dead. It was this look that gave rise to Glock's unofficial nickname, 'Ghostly Glock', although never in public and certainly never to his face. His large, bulbous forehead supported a framework of wiry, grey hair, which he would scrape back and slick down with thick applications of an obnoxious smelling pomade. His sunken eyes sockets housed steely-grey rheumy eyes, that darted about in a perpetual state of watery awareness. Hollowed out cheeks gave way to a viciously pointed chin, which framed a thin letterbox mouth that seemed to have a permanent collection of sticky white spittle pooling in the corners. His very presence conjured up death and decay. Thousands of unfortunate souls who crossed his path were soon to discover at his hands, their lives became a living Purgatory.

For the past few years, the Nazis had been busy building new labour camps which had now started to appear throughout the German occupied territories. Those who were unfortunate enough to be sent to them, mistakenly believed they were being spared death. In reality they were being delivered to several of Glock's preferred hunting grounds. He would sweep in on unscheduled visits with a detachment of Stormtroopers, selecting up to fifty people at a time and transferring them to secret SS facilities. It wasn't long before they wished they had been left to face their chances at the hands of the sadistic camp commandant's. Once Glock had got his hands on them, the most they could hope for was a quick death, but rarely did any of them receive one. Many eyewitness accounts would place him as a frequent visitor to Treblinka, Dachau and of course Auschwitz. Ghostly Glock's reputation had elevated him as the Party's 'Reich Necromancer,' and he embraced the accolade with a morbid satisfaction and unnatural skill.

It took less than a minute before a thin reedy voice spoke at the end of the line.

"Good evening Heinrich, I trust you are well?" He enquired with the breathy wheeze. It was more of a statement than a question.

"Herr General." Major Schaffer jumped, snapping out of his own thoughts the instant Glock's voice came on the line. "I am sorry to bother you sir however, I thought you should know I'm calling from Werner's office."

There was a moment's pause in conversation with the only audible noise that could be heard was the mucoid breathing of Glock's rasping breath, then a very deliberate reply was precisely delivered to the major.

"Did I not give specific orders for that department to be shut down, Major?" Glock had a knack of making a casual observation sound like a direct threat. A cold chill ran down Heinrich's spine and not just because Glock used his Christian name, something which always bothered him.

"My apologies Herr General." Schaffer squirmed. "You did sir, and your orders have been carried out." The major unconsciously tugged at his shirt collar. Glock continued to speak.

"Yet you are calling me from Hauptmann Fuchs's office." Another pause before he added. "Is this correct Major?"

Heinrich spluttered into the mouthpiece, a prickly heat rising up the entire length of his body.

"That is correct General. The last item to be collected was Werner's…Hauptmann Fuchs's desk. This is scheduled for 08:00 hours tomorrow. Five minutes ago, I received a call from Wewelsburg Castle on this line." He paused for a moment before adding. "In Paderborn."

"I am perfectly aware of the location of Wewelsburg Castle, thank you very much Major." Glock sneered.

"Yes sir. I thought you would wish to know the nature of the telephone phone call?" Schaffer asked.

Another wheeze emanated from the earpiece of the receiver. "Continue."

"Von Riker has established a link. The device has been activated and Paderborn has replied. We have communications with our agent. Project Zeitsprung…It's working Herr General."

This news cemented Glock's attention. He paused for just the right amount of time as he absorbed what the Major had just said, before delivering a curt reply.

"Major, assemble your team and collect me from the Reich Ministry. We go to Wewelsburg tonight." The call was terminated with an abrupt click.

"Ja Voll" Sturmbannführer Schaffer said looking at the disconnected receiver before replacing it on the cradle.

He perched on the corner of the loan desk for a while, looking around the empty office before exhaling an exasperated breath through a set of pursed lips. He removed his peaked cap and taking a clean pressed handkerchief from his trouser pocket, he dabbed the perspiration from his forehead. Schaffer stood and made for the exit, stopping to ensure he locked the door on his way out.

"My God." Heinrich muttered to himself. "I do not have a good feeling about this." He replaced the key to the office in his tunic pocket and retreated at a quickened pace, heading back down the corridor.

Heinrich Schaffer was a professional soldier. He knew much about military tactics and the conventional business of war. He was also smart enough to recognise that what he was getting involved with was by no means natural or proper. The conversation he'd just had didn't sit right with him.

"KRUPPS!" He shouted as he approached the duty officer's mess.

A round-faced sergeant poked his head from an open-door frame. He was wearing a non-regulation white napkin stuffed into the collar of his tunic.

"Put down the pastries my fat friend." Heinrich said as he approached. "We have just been activated. Project Zeitsprung has come online. We are to collect ghostly, erm, Obergruppenführer Glock and make our way to Paderborn."

Krupps greeted the news with widening eyes. His ever-open mouth dispensed a patisserie avalanche of half chewed strudel that bounced off the scuffed toe caps of his boots.

"Mouth shut, Krupps." The Major said as he brushed past, pushing the sergeant's jaw up with two fingers. "It is the least attractive of your qualities, to which you possess very few."

Krupps continued to gape, wordlessly mouthing his astonishment at the news the major had just delivered.

Heinrich paused for just a moment and looked at the sergeant, sighing with obvious disappointment.

"Krupps." he said. "To my knowledge the light and fluffy casings of those pastries you constantly cram down that cavernous gullet of yours, have never been known to become airborne. Therefore, the only thing you're in danger of swallowing right now is a passing family of flies. Talking of which, yours are open. Button yourself up Sergeant, we have work to do."

There was a mad scrabbling from Krupps as he adjusted his dishevelled uniform, smearing whipped cream from his fingers all over his groin. By the time he had brushed most of it away the major was almost at the motor pool. In the remaining seconds that it took for the news to penetrate the fat layers around Krupps's brain, the Major had the door open and was standing in the open air.

"Fresh pretzels to the first one in the car." He teased. Krupps needed no further encouragement. Grabbing the napkin in his hand and yanking it clear from his neck, the rotund sergeant put on a surprising turn of speed as he raced after Major Schaffer.

"Good heavens, Krupps." The Major exclaimed. "You resemble all the characteristics of a heavy goods vehicle. You don't so much as accelerate as get underway."

The thin white linen cloth that had been keeping the flakes of pastry from infiltrating Krupps's multiple neck layers, had barely enough time to float to the ground by the time he was at the exit of the door. Pushing past Heinrich, he made a beeline at maximum speed towards a military grey staff car. He opened the driver's side door of the Kübelwagen and irreverently threw himself into the seat, a triumphant look on his sweating brow. The Major watched from the doorway, smiling to himself as the automobile's suspension audibly gasped in its struggle to compensate for the sudden increase in weight. Using the tips of his thumb and forefinger, Krupps deftly stuffed the remaining corner of the half-eaten strudel into his mouth, sucking at the sausage like digits so as to ensure that he savoured every last morsel. He pushed up the peak of his forage cap and beckoned the Major over.

"Krupps, my fat friend." Schaffer said, as he climbed into the back of the vehicle. "It seems evident to me that the American's won't need to waste a bullet on you. All Eisenhower has to do is wait for you to eat yourself to death."

Krupps grunted as he swallowed.

"However, before we allow the Allied supreme commander that chance, perhaps you can manage to get us to the Reich Ministry? In a manner keeping in style with how you like to consume your elevenses…preferably in one piece."

Krupps craned his head a fraction, smiling at the Major he turned the ignition key. At the second attempt the engine spluttered into life. Krupps wrapped a sticky hand around the gear shifter and supplemented by much graunching, thrashed about until he found a gear to engage.

"I'm pretty sure they make these things with a clutch." Schaffer observed from the back seat.

A loud 'Clunk' announced Krupps had been successful in his search for the elusive gear. He lifted his boot off the clutch pedal and slammed the other onto the gas. With a violent lurch, the vehicle and its two occupants shot out of the courtyard, accompanied by an orchestration of screeching tyres and a billowing blue-white cloud of burning rubber, which mixed with the coiling exhaust fumes left hanging over the courtyard in the still April air.

WEWELSBURG CASTLE

SS PARANORMAL DIVISIONAL HEADQUARTERS

Twelve hours later, in one of the many anti-rooms deep in the heart of Wewelsburg Castle, Obergruppenführer Glock, Sturmbannführer Schaffer and Staff Sergeant Krupps sat in the company of two shadowy figures, both dressed in civilian clothing. Each of the civilian men wore the ubiquitous party pin on his lapel and had the unmistakable whiff of the Geheime Staatspolizei about them. The feared secret police, more commonly referred to by their street name, The Gestapo.

"Gentlemen." The taller of the two plain clothed figures announced in greeting. "Allow me to introduce myself. My name is Herr Stöller and this is my colleague, Herr Lanz." He indicated to Lanz with a casual wave of his hands. Stöller was a heavy-set bulldog of a man. He was completely bald with a thick roll of fat surrounding the back of his head. Although he shaved twice a day he still had a permanent blue sheen to his anvil jaw. The steely edge to his voice ensured that nobody enquired as to his credentials. Everybody present around the table nodded their greetings to one another. Once all the introductions were out of the way, Herr Stöller continued.

"Some of you will be aware by now that at 22:01 hours and 15 seconds exactly, on the evening of April 12, 1943, Project Zeitsprung was successfully activated."

Schaffer rolled his eyes. "You can always trust the Gestapo to be so precise." He thought as he listened to the briefing. It was clear that Schaffer had little in the way of respect towards the Gestapo. To his mind any policeman was bad enough, let alone the Secret Police. As far as Schaffer was concerned, they were just a bunch of brutes with badges. Now would not be the best time to show his dislike for their profession. He needed to bide his time. Though he imagined Ghostly Glock would be revelling in this meticulously delivered exactitude. Schaffer wondered how much longer he was going to have to sit here for and listen to this officious policeman. He checked his watch and was annoyed to discover that it had stopped. He tapped the glass bezel and lifted it to his ear. "Damned Dusseldorf rubbish. Next time, Swiss." He muttered.

Krupps, meanwhile was eying up a large pile of sticky croissants that had been placed on the table, a fingertips distance out of his reach. Jugs of steaming hot coffee were passed around, which meant Herr Stöller was temporarily obliged to pause his speech until the chiming of silver against porcelain died down. Once the distraction of refreshments abated, the Gestapo man continued.

"I want you all to realise that there can be little doubt," he said with a serious expression, "this is no hoax. Neither is it a false alarm. In a secure room within this castle, our most brilliant scientists are waiting to share with you a discovery that will ensure a glorious victory over the Allied forces." He stopped to take on board everybody's reactions. Satisfied that he had complete command of the room he pressed home his advantage. "Yesterday the bait was taken. Tonight, we reel in our little fish and see what we have caught."

There was a buzz of nervous excitement in the room. The Gestapo man had the quality of a showman about him. Schaffer imagined that if Himmler ever tired of him, he would certainly get a job with Goebbels propaganda ministry. Stöller interrupted Schaffer's thoughts by pulling out a silver pocket watch, engraved with an endearing inscription from the head of the Criminal Police Division himself; Arthur Nebe. He pressed the release catch and watched as the lid flipped open. A melody played out. Schaffer recognised the short extract from Wagner's Ring Cycle opera, Götterdämmerung. "How apt." Schaffer mumbled to himself. "The downfall of the gods. Valhalla engulfed in flames. These crazy paranormal assholes are going to do the same thing to us very probably."

With a sharp snap Stöller closed the lid, severing Schaffer's reverie.

"It is time." He announced as he stood up, scraping the chair over the stone floor. "You will follow me and we shall begin."

Stöller turned on his heels and marched smartly out of the room, followed by the entourage of senior SS officers and a round faced staff Sergeant, who by now had bulging tunic pockets and was licking his fingers.

CHAPTER 3

APRIL, LONDON 2016

David woke to find himself sprawled on the floor of his bedroom. He had no idea how long he had been out. He lifted an arm to check his watch, it felt heavy. He peered at the dial through the half-gloom that struggled to light his dingy room, his brain was struggling to cope with its returning senses. Dawn was beginning to win the inevitable battle over the night's claim, pushing the first fingers of its ochre rays over the rooftops and creeping onto the waking faces of the city. He managed to squint his eyes to bring the blurred dial into focus. The hands pointed to 22:01. Still stopped. He shook his wrist and tapped the glass face, before holding it up to his ear...nothing. "Another useless piece of junk that shopkeeper has given me." He thought. "So much for German quality timepieces. I should have got a Swiss one."

David grabbed hold of the side of his bed and struggled to his feet, a wave of nausea passed over his body. For a moment he thought his legs would buckle underneath him. He thrust out a steadying hand. His head was spinning in all directions. Vague memories danced about the fractured boundaries of his mind like the shattered shards of a mirror. He screwed his face up in a ghastly grimace. The pulsating dull ache in his head shifted in intensity, downgrading to a steady throb. Images danced a fingertip away from his consciousness, weaving their way between a dream-like state to full cognitive recall before being snatched away again. After a minute or two, his traumatised mind started to win the fight and the hazy recollections of last night gradually began to coalesce in the swirling mental fog. Enticing glimpses began to crystalise and give birth to solid forms in ever sharper clarity. As the minutes passed, more pieces started to come back to him, becoming less like a bad dream and more like a waking nightmare. Still blinking in the gloom, David saw the box nestling where he had left it, the vivid blood red etchings standing out in a macabre contrast to the porcelain white background. The instant David caught sight of the box; all reservations of his reality dissolved instantly. This was no dream.

"Okay, so that actually happened then." He said to himself.

David felt another memory stirring deep within his subconsciousness. Something to do with his hands. He lifted them up to his face and squinted at them. He saw the scattering of red dots marking his skin. Dark stains on his palms indicated where his blood had pooled before drying out. Rusty red crusts flaked off as he clenched his fists. He began pumping them to see if he was still leaking...he wasn't. David felt like an addict waking from a drug-fuelled coma. It was as if his body was wracked with pain and discomfort from a noxiously imbibed substance still swimming through the bloodstream, yet like an addict craving more junk, David found that he was still being drawn to the mystical allure of the box. He was hooked! He stared at the box, a mixture of intrigue and mistrust playing out across his face.

"What are you?" What do you do?" He stopped in his tracks and let out a long sigh.

"Great, now you have me talking to myself. Whatever you are, I don't have time for this right now."

He looked at his watch again, then groaned. "But I do have time for a new watch." A noise coming from downstairs reminded him that he wasn't alone in the house, "and I had better get that creeping barrage balloon some rent, before I'm thrown out on the street."

An hour later, David found himself stood on the street outside his bank. In his hand he fingered a well-used bankcard, which he offered up to the slot of an ATM machine. He keyed in his four-digit security code and waited for the menu to come up on the screen. He selected the... 'Check My Balance' option and shuffled back and forth on his feet, performing a nervous shimmy as the ATM issued its instructions.

'Please Wait'

With a sterile beep, a message flashed up...

'YOUR ACCOUNT BALANCE IS... OVERDRAWN -£78.00'

Declining the offer of choosing another service, David asked for his card back, which the ATM obliged with a vulgar noise. David couldn't help but feel the disappointment, despite already knowing the outcome of his futile effort. While deciding on his next course of action he remembered part of the shopkeeper's conversation... 'David, you say you cannot afford to buy this box, but I say you cannot afford NOT to buy it. You are studying history, are you not? You are not purchasing a trinket. This isn't any ordinary box and, if used correctly it could be your ticket to financial independence. Trust me when I say……..you need this box, David'...

"David? David! Hang on, the shopkeeper called me David. How did he know my name?"

It was only a few streets away from the bank, but the next thing David realised was seeing his reflection staring back at him from a plate-glass window. He must have made the short journey on automatic pilot, so when he found himself standing on the opposite kerb looking directly at the antique shop, he decided that he would seize the moment and confront the crazy old man and find out what was happening to him. He placed one foot onto the road and was about to cross when an unseen hand grabbed the back of his collar and yanked him clear, just as a truck thundered past his face.

"Bitte. You need to be more careful, young man. Your life is more valuable than you know." A soft accented voice said.

David turned to meet his saviour and found himself gazing into a pair of emerald green eyes, framed by the round ruddy face of a portly old man. There were remnants of a freshly devoured chocolate éclair still evident on his face.

"Thank you." David stammered.

"Ihr Willkommen." The man replied, a kindly smile on his face. "Now, if you'll excuse me, I have to be getting on." The rotund old gentleman squeezed David's shoulder with a powerful wrinkled hand. "Look after yourself mein freund, my employer wishes no harm to come to you".

"No, wait...I......" The words David wanted remained buried and all he could manage was a dry croak.

"Your employer?" David thought. "What is happening to me today? Who are these people?" He needed answers and gave chase.

For such a large figure, the man had managed to cross the street and was at the entrance to the shop with a surprising turn of speed. This time David looked up and down the road with caution before pursuing the man across the street. He caught up with him as the old man fumbled with the lock of the door to the antiques shop. David narrowed the gap calling out moments before the man had the chance to close the door. He jammed his foot into the doorway as the door swung shut.

"Please." He implored to the old man. Then with a small whimper. "Ouch, my foot!" Recovering a little decorum, he blurted out a fusillade of questions. "I have to know. Who are you and who is your employer? And why do you both care so much about my wellbeing? Where do you know me from? We have never met, have we?"

There was a commotion coming from inside the shop. A figure appeared behind the portly man. David recognised the shopkeeper as he placed his hands on the man's shoulder and guided him into the shop. "It's okay Gunther, I'll take it from here. Go on in and put the kettle on."

The fat man looked at David with kindly eyes. "Auf Wiedersehen, David. See you soon." He said, before departing into the shop.

The shopkeeper took up his vacant position in the doorway. "Hello, young man. What can I help you with?" he enquired.

David swallowed hard before drawing himself up to his full 5ft 6inches and spoke in a timorous voice. "I've been passing your shop every day for the past 6 months. Yesterday, you sold me a box. Last night I used it and now strange things are happening to me. I don't want the box anymore. I can't afford it anyway. I'm in trouble with my landlady and I need to pay my rent but stupidly, I gave you the last of my wages for that box. And another thing, I didn't think much about it at the time, but you called me by my name, I never told you what my name was. How do you know me, how do you know my name?

The old man brought his hand up and cupped David's cheek, his fingers were ice cold. There was a sadness in his eyes that betrayed his denial of knowing David.

"Do not concern yourself with such things. It does not matter how I know your name young David. Probably from your bank card when you were in here purchasing the box?"

"I paid cash" David countered.

"A lucky guess perhaps"? The shopkeeper winked at David after saying this. "It's what you are about to do that's important. So, I must be going. We will meet again where I will be able to tell you more, however, now is not the right time. I have to be sure that you carry out your task without interference by me, or anyone else. Goodbye for now young David and good luck, son".

With that, the Shopkeeper shut the door. There was the sound of bolts being slid into their receivers before he pulled down a roller blind, which prevented David from seeing the old man disappear into the gloom of the shop interior.

David looked at his reflection in the glass of the shop door. "No rent for Mrs Reynolds today then". He sighed out loud as he shuffled back along the high street. He thrust his hands into his coat pockets and felt a small piece of cardboard. "Funny". He thought, "that wasn't there before".

Pulling it out, he found a ripped fragment of a crumpled business card, yellowed and torn with frayed edges. There was just enough lettering on it to make out the words.

'Rei...Anti....Est.. 194..Pro...H. Mey......'

On the reverse of the card were a few letters in dark pencil, but nothing that made any sense. David's thoughts returned to the box and the mysteries it held. With little prospect of getting hold of any cash before the end of the day, David decided to make the short journey back to his lodgings, while he could legitimately claim that he still lived there. There was just over a week left to go before his wages were due. For the past two years David had managed to juggle his university studies with his job as an assistant librarian. David's meagre salary wasn't about to make him rich. He'd just have to dodge Mrs Reynolds for a few more days, a skill he was becoming quite adept in.

David let himself in as quietly as he could and tiptoed past his landlady's door. He glided silently through the hallway and almost floated to the bottom of the stairs. He lifted his foot deliberately to miss out treading on the second step. After months of trying to evade the unwanted attentions of his landlady, he had built a mental map of all the areas he knew wouldn't emit any noise and deliberately avoided treading on those that would wake the slumbering dragon. He managed to make it halfway up the stairs before the lounge door swung open and the frame was filled by the corpulent figure of his arch nemesis. Her flowery one-piece linen frock billowed gently in the spring breeze, which struggled to find a gap to flow around. The air that did make it past carried with it the pungent aroma of carbolic soap and lavender water to David's nostrils.

Mrs Reynolds had her arms folded across her ample bosom, the pudgy flesh and loose skin sagged from her forearms and hung down, losing its battle against gravity. Her once flowing hair had long since given up its lustrous ebony shine. Instead, the jet-black curls were now taken over by the advancing threads of dark, silvery grey. She regarded her recalcitrant lodger from behind the thick frames of a pair of horn-rimmed spectacles, nestling on the tip of a ruddy nose. Her mordant gaze was powerful enough to freeze her quarry in mid-flight.

"David"? she asked in the tone of a reproaching school mistress. "Have you anything for me today"? She extended one arm out horizontally, her fleshy palm pointing upwards while her fingers curled back and forth in a beckoning gesture.

David hesitated before he answered her. "Oh, erm...yes. Mrs Reynolds, I know that I said that...err... Well, what I meant was that...umm, you see, the thing is, there's this thing...err, I'm sure you know about it...oh, and umm...Gosh, would you look at the time?"

Tapping his broken watch, David inched up the stairs the way a hunter would back away from a very large and dangerous predator...with great care and respect. The moment his foot stepped onto the landing, he turned on his heels and bolted along the short corridor, darting into his room and slamming the door behind him. He slumped backwards against it; his chest heaving as he gulped down lungful's of air. Grasping behind, his fingers found the key where upon he frantically turned it, shooting the bolt across with a metallic, 'Clunk!'

Mrs Reynolds remained in the doorway; her arm still outstretched before resigning herself to a sigh of disappointment. She turned on her slippered heels and retreated back into her living room.

"Such a shame about that boy," she tutted to herself. "Always used to be such a nice young man."

She continued to mutter something about the youth of today not being as it was in her generation but the door swung closed, cutting off anymore of her disenchanted mutterings.

Now David was safely locked in his room, he walked over to the table and pulled off the blanket that covered the box. He grabbed hold of the stool and plonked himself down. His hands hovered a few centimetres over the surface. He interweaved his fingers together and extended them out, his knuckles cracking like splintering wood. He reached out five tentative fingertips for the floating planchette. There was a slight electrical feeling beginning to emanate from the box which David could feel running up and down the surface of his skin, it made the hairs on his forearms stand vertically. When his fingers were within an inch or two from the triangular shape, the planchette leapt into his grip with a suddenness that took him by surprise.

"Okay." He said to the box, "Let's see what you're all about".

The box hummed in David's ears without seeming to emit any physical noise. The static charge continued to creep along David's fingers, tingling as it advanced along his arms and down into his torso. An electric-blue glow had enveloped him from head to toe, surrounding him with a spectral aurora. His whole body crackled with the positive charge of an energy source not naturally found in the normal world, and one that had no business belonging in David's bedroom.

CHAPTER 4

APRIL 1943 – WEWELSBURG CASTLE

SS PARANORMAL DIVISIONAL HEADQUARTERS

Deep within the basement of Himmler's operational castle was a vaulted room known as the "Hall of the Dead." It consisted of a circular chamber with twelve low stone platforms around its walls. In the centre was an altar, designed for black worship. This alter was the focal point of the room where frantic attempts were made by a secret cult called: 'The Order' to invoke the dark, mystical powers of the 'Black Sun'. Twelve Knight initiates would stand on each of the stone platforms against the walls facing the central altar, and would attempt to channel psychic power to the high priest. These SS ceremonies required human blood sacrifice, which was not a problem; the SS concentration camps and prisons were full of them. A small group of sacrificial victims were kept at the castle for this very purpose.

The cabal of senior officers were seated at a round mahogany table in the hall. The warm spring temperatures outside were a pleasing change to the harsh winters of 41-42. Inside the thick walls of the castle however, a unique set of environmental circumstances transformed their hot breath into vapour clouds, which hung in an exhaled suspension above their heads. A lingering odour of decaying tobacco smoke scented the room, layering the air in undulating sheets. The aromatic soup was gently circulated around the room by a slowly rotating ceiling fan, which agitated the fetid mixture and added to it the stench of sweat and unwashed bodies. Fingers of black mildew rose up to meet the rivulets of condensation that trickled down the whitewashed stone walls. Pools of stagnant water collected on the uneven flagstones, reflecting the occupants of the room like a malevolent black mirror. The room was lit by four gantry lights which cast a yellow tinged hue against the walls and ceiling.

Five pairs of eyes were fixed on a brooding object that sat in the centre of the altar. A large rectangular box, roughly the size of a Monopoly game board, with a grey metallic base, glass sides and a milk-white opaque polished surface. The box hummed gently to itself. A sixth man joined the group. This man was not wearing a military uniform. His suit was of medium quality, as were his scuffed brogues. He wore a plain black tie over a white cotton shirt and the final garment, the ultimate giveaway as to what part he played in this charade, was a slightly ill-fitting lab coat; ubiquitously found adorning scientists the world over.

The man walked over to an array of cumbersome looking scientific instruments, which had been arranged in a hastily constructed tower against the back wall of the room. He paid no attention to the precariousness of the stack, preferring instead to check some of the readings the machinery was registering. Flicking a few switches and turning the odd dial or two, he muttered something technical sounding to himself that would probably have been unintelligible to the rest of the group, even if they had managed to hear him. The man retrieved a clipboard from underneath his right arm and made what appeared to be the appropriate notes for the occasion. With well-practiced moves he referred back to the dials and gauges, tapping them now and again with the end of an expensive looking fountain pen; by way of reassuring himself that they were reading correctly. This also introduced an element of theatre to the easily impressed minds of his audience. With a slow, deliberate precision, the scientist turned around from the whirring array of devices and regarded each of the seated men; their eyes now diverted from the box and firmly fixed upon him.

On the table in front of each man was a manila folder secured by a large wax circle bearing the official seal of Reichsführer Himmler's office. Two words stamped below in large red letters simply red...

STRENG GEHIME

(TOP SECRET)

"Guten Tag, allow me to introduce myself. For those of you who do not already know me, my name is Professor Horst von Riker. I am the senior lead scientist for 'Project Zeitsprung'."

Had he been wearing a pair of gold-rimmed spectacles he would have chosen this moment to peer over their frames; he wasn't. Instead his cold lazuli eyes pierced through the dusty half-light of the basement room, fixing each attendee with a frozen stare.

"Before I continue, you have all been summoned here by order of Reichsführer Himmler. Each and every one of you in this room have been granted the security clearance of Black-Ultra. What you are about to hear is highly classified. Which means that what is discussed here today remains within the confines of this room. You are to speak of this meeting with no one outside of these walls. Is that clear?"

Each man looked at the other with narrowing eyes. A gentle murmur was all anyone could manage. Von Riker spoke again, this time a little more forcefully.

"Is that clear, gentlemen?"

This time their reply was more verbose.

"Ya, ya…it is clear."

Von Riker continued. "Please pick up the folders before you and break the seals."

There was a moment of frenetic rustling as they picked up the folders and ripped off the waxed ribbon sealing the contents.

"You will see yesterday evening we successfully made contact with the counterpart to the box that sits before us today. If you read the files in front of you, you will see that this is one of two identical boxes; we call this one Box A."

Major Schaffer shifted awkwardly in his seat. He brought up his hand to his mouth and allowed a small cough to escape his lips. "Two boxes you say? Then where is the other box Herr Professor?"

Von Riker's head snapped around to locate the source of this interruption to his oratory, the icy focus of his eyes zeroed in and fixed upon the Major. In a sepulchre voice he said.

"Not where Sturmbannführer Schaffer...When!"

An uncomfortable silence returned to the room, allowing von Riker to continue.

"A few days ago...that is to say a few days as far as we are concerned, the glorious Reich's elite PSD, placed the other box...Box B, in a specially designed chamber built beneath the Black Mountains, where it was bombarded with an intense burst of super accelerated chroniton particles."

"PSD?" Somebody questioned.

Riker snorted before clarifying. "SS Paranormal Scientific Division. P..S..D."

"Why?" This time the interruption came from General Glock.

Von Riker adjusted the level of his annoyance at being interrupted again. When he saw who had asked the question he stiffened, ever so slightly. He gripped the lapels of his lab coat and launched into an enthusiastic explanation.

"Chroniton Particle Research is the theoretical study of Chroniton Particles and their effect on the Space/Time Continuum. Chroniton Particles are a sub-atomic particle with temporal properties which exist in a state of temporal flux. We have long suspected that Chroniton particles can be artificially manufactured and stored within the magnetic confines of an interphasic generator. When an object is exposed to a steady stream of these particles it will undergo temporal polarisation, the molecules of the object become 'phased'. In other words, they co-exist on two planes of the Space/Time continuum at the same time. If we then subject this phased object to an intense burst of microscopic forced energy, we can redirect its path through the temporal continuum. Essentially making an exact duplicate of the first box and allowing it to travel through time."

"Theoretical?" Glock questioned.

"Gentlemen. I am pleased to report that as of last night, this research is no longer theoretical. Box B was successfully projected into the future. We can estimate the distance it has travelled by analysing the decay rate of the sub atomic particles and calculate the time dilation. We call this the Schism. Regrettably it is not an exact science, but we confidently estimate a time-jump of 75 to 80 years, plus or minus a few months either side. The schism fluctuates naturally all the time."

"How frustrating that must be to a man like you." Schaffer scoffed under his breath. Before von Riker could react to the remark, Glock cut him off with more questions.

"This is quite remarkable, Herr Riker. So, you are saying that we have established a connecting time line to the second box. What happens next, can we send a man forward in time too?" Glock pressed the scientist as the potential of what had been said began to sink in.

Von Riker readjusted the grip he had on his coat lapels and half-turned away from Schaffer, straight into the inquisitive stare of Glock. He cleared his throat and continued.

"To be honest with you there was no way of knowing whether the experiment had been a success or not. We believe chroniton particles are harmless to human beings, sending a live specimen through time though is not yet within our capabilities. We weren't even sure if we could transmute an inanimate object until yesterday. However, when Box B began transmitting, we knew we had established a connection with our agent."

"Agent?" Glock questioned. "From the future? So, you have sent someone through."

"Nein, Herr General. We had to do it the long way round. We waited for the agent living at that time to initiate the connection back to us. This is where trying to explain time travel can quickly become very complicated. Do not worry too much, Herr General, about the specifics. Suffice to say that the PSD have a trusted member loyal to the SS who is guiding and controlling matters in the future."

Glock gave a sideways glance at Schaffer. Major Schaffer noticed this brief exchange and averted his gaze.

Himmler's Paranormal Scientific Division held a mixture of intrigue and fear throughout the Wehrmacht. Most of the soldiers fighting on the front lines had heard rumours of strange things coming out of Wewelsburg. Stories would be told at night during a lull in fighting, usually around a burning brazier, and would filter through the ranks. Officers were under orders to dismiss these tales as superstitious propaganda. Stories devised to frighten the enemy.

This didn't dissuade the soldiers need to tell stories though. Reports emerged from soldiers returning from the NAZI outpost in Antarctica. They would entertain their comrades in the mess hall with tall fantastic tales about flying machines shaped like gigantic bells, which could float over the ice without making a noise and hover in a manner that defied gravity. New NAZI propulsion systems capable of driving a craft without a propeller at speeds beyond anything currently flying in the skies at the time.

Another popular story doing the rounds in the mess halls, concerned a mystical power source called; 'The Vril', which was said to be capable of creating a force of such unimaginable destruction, that it could vanquish the mightiest of enemies and lay waste to their lands with a single thought.

But, the most persistent story and by far the troops favourite, was the rumour surrounding a squadron of biologically engineered super soldiers. Men who had artificially enhanced endurance and held no fear in the face of the enemy.

Just one squadron of these 'Wonder Soldiers' were said to have captured a fortified Allied position without being affected by their weapons. An Obergefreiter serving with the 24th Panzer Division, claimed to have witnessed the assault. "They are unstoppable. It took only half a dozen of these Red-Eyed Devils to wipe out an entire brigade of enemy troops. Machine gun bullets and grenades just passed through their bodies, which then repaired itself in front of the enemy's eyes."

Back in the castle, Von Riker's pride swelled further as he became carried away in his own hyperbole.

"Today we will find out what the future holds for the glorious thousand year reign our Führer has always promised the people of the Third Reich. Only committed members of the National Socialist German Workers Party will benefit from this clear example of Germany's determination and superior intellect. What we say today will soon be forgotten. What we do will live on for a thousand, thousand years. Today we don't just make history...Today we alter it. Heil Hitler". Von Riker thrust his chin out and brought the heels of his brogues together emitting a loud click, which echoed throughout the cavernous qualities of the vault. He extended his right hand outward, issuing a crisp salute that pleased General Glock.

The reverberations of a ceremonial gong rang out, initiating the beginnings of Von Riker's ritual. The others looked on as twelve men filed into the hall in complete silence. They were dressed in plain white cotton robes bearing the SS rune symbol on the breast. Each man took his place on top of the twelve platforms with devout observation and turned to face the centre of the room. Two SS guards followed behind, dragging a wretched figure. One of the hapless prisoners plucked from the castle's dungeons. A pentagram of Demonic worship had been laid into the stone floor. At the tip of each mosaic point a burning candle cast a flickering light. They positioned the barely conscious victim in the middle of the effigy and exited the hall.

Von Riker walked over to the altar and gave one last look around the room. He took a deep breath before placing his hands on the surface of the box. A steel swishing noise filled the room. The four electric lamps that had been burning steadily began to flicker and dim, until all they managed to emit was a pulsating orange glow, before winking out altogether. Von Riker's eyes rolled back in their sockets his head snapped forward with a sudden lurch. The black power surging through his body, violently flung his head backwards with a force that would normally snap a man's neck. He blinked and opened his eyes to reveal two cloudy opaque orbs with no obvious irises or visible pupils. He stared blindly at the room, murmuring sightlessly to himself. Five blades retracted back into channels hidden in the Demonic design, leaving a pool of bright red blood draining from the exsanguinated body lying on the floor. The blood was divided into five rivulets and drained into holes at the tips of the pentagram.

Major Schaffer looked away, barely concealing his horror. If he hadn't had doubts before, he was beginning to develop serious reservations about his involvement, especially after the gory ceremony he had just witnessed. He decided to keep them to himself. He retrieved a small card from his pocket. Picking up a pencil from the table he scribbled a hasty note on the reverse just before the light failed altogether.

840 miles away and 73 years into the future, a message began to appear on an identical box in David's bedroom. His eyes were two milky white orbs with no irises or pupils.

CHAPTER 5

LONDON 2016

The planchette glided effortlessly in David's fingers, the crystal disc lingering for less than a second over each letter and spelling out a contemporaneous message from the past. A two-way conversation separated by time, yet linked like a supernatural long distance telephone call. Neither David, nor von Riker actually read the letters as they were being spelled out. The box managed to communicate the message directly into the operator's mind using occult telepathy. The result was a seemingly normal conversation between two people, the reality was much more disconcerting to anyone observing.

"David, tell me. What year is this?" Von Riker asked from 1943.

"2016.' David replied, adding. "April 23rd."

"And what news of the thousand-year Reich? Is our dear Fuhrers beloved dream of National Socialism still alive?

Even cocooned in a semi trance-like state, this question still managed to have a sobering effect on David.

"Thousand year what? Fuhrer? What the hell have I got here?" He thought. The moment he formed the words in his mind, the box transmitted them back to von Riker, with a disquieting effect. An instant later, another volley of questions played out across the surface of the box. "How was our glorious victory celebrated? What year did our mighty forces prevail? What of the evil oppressors, the Capitalist pig-dogs in the west and those Communist red savages in the East? Have they been vanquished?"

The questions came over in relentless waves, each one increasing in its passion, as if von Rikers own ideological belief fuelled the intensity and elevated its power through telepathic transference. David's mind was swamped by von Riker's ethereal presence.

"ENOUGH!" David screamed. He tried to push away from the table but the box wouldn't release its grip. His eyes briefly flickered back to normal, but the box regained its grip. David's eyes once again clouded over. He instantly calmed down and resumed his paranormal conversation.

"The Germans lost the war!" He transmitted. There was an uneasy delay before an incredulous explosion of demands flowed over the box.

"What! How can this be? Who beat us, was it those cowardly Cossacks? Or those good-time Charlies, the Americans? Von Riker challenged.

Horst von Riker's words hung over both tables in both timelines. In the castle, spectral emanations rose from the surface of the box, adding to the frigid atmosphere already present in the basement vault. A paranormal iciness that penetrated deep into the bone. The rivulets of condensation that had been running down the walls had turned to a glistening sheet of ice. The pools of water were now frozen solid. Schaffer grabbed the lapels of his tunic and bunching them together drew in his jacket tighter, in an effort to ward off the cold. He cupped his hands to his mouth and exhaled a long stream of dragon's breath, desperately trying to warm his freezing fingers. Schaffer shuddered "Is it just me or has it got a lot colder in here?" The other men were all shivering, with the exception of Ghostly Glock, who was fixated on Von Riker's face.

The box continued to spell out letters from David's future. "You got your Nazi asses handed to you by...well, by everyone in the end. The Russians, the Americans, the British. In fact, pretty much every country in the free world. The Japanese surrendered 3 months later. Years later, one or two Japanese soldiers would pop up on remote islands in the Pacific and threaten the odd tourist with a rusty bayonet, but only because no one had told them that the world was no longer at war."

"There must be some mistake?" von Riker interrupted "You are playing some kind of joke on me...that is it, isn't it?"

"No mistake and no joke either. Oh, and do you want to know what happened to your Fuhrer?" David asked.

"Yes, yes!" Came an eager reply.

"On the 30th April 1945, the leader of your Third Reich married his girlfriend Eva Braun, then shot her. Then he turned the gun on himself and put a bullet in his own head, while the Russians were knocking on the doors of Berlin. Seven days later Germany surrendered, unconditionally."

"Impossible! There is no way we could have lost." von Riker spluttered.

David continued. "Goebbels poisoned his entire family, Goering poisoned himself, as did Himmler in the hands of his captors. I would say that constitutes as losing, wouldn't you agree?"

"There is no way we are going to lose. Our forces are stronger; our equipment is far superior to anything that the Allies have. Our generals will ensure that we prevail." von Riker was spitting with rage.

"Will this be the same generals who ordered fifty gallons of petrol to be poured over the Fuhrer's corpse and burned Mrs & Mrs H in a shallow ditch outside the Berlin bunker? Or are you thinking of some different generals?"

"I do not care for your tone, neither do I believe in your lies...I refuse to believe them." von Riker insisted.

"Have it your own way fritz, but I'm here in 2016 and I can tell you the Nazi Party died, along with old Adolf back in 1945. There was no thousand years, no glorious march to victory. Most of those who didn't join Adolf taking the coward's way out, met their fate at the end of an Allied noose. But don't stress. It's all sweet now, because we're friends with the German's...We drive their cars and everything." David added this last statement as an afterthought, as he realised that he was being a bit harsh on his new friend from the past, Nazi or otherwise.

There was a slight pause in the flow of the conversation and then a new presence was felt over the board. Someone else had taken control and joined the party. David asked himself if it were possible to physically feel malice. The planchette began to dance over the letters again with a renewed urgency.

"David, my name is Herr Glock, I am one of '*those*' Generals you speak of in the SS." Claus Glock over-pronounced the alliteration of both 'S's' so they sounded like a hissing snake. "So far you have given us a glimpse into one possible future, but now you and I are going to change all that and I am going to instruct you how you are going to do this, is that understood, David?

David laughed to himself. "This totally crazy box is something else. Here I am about to take orders from a Nazi general who has long been dead and buried in the ground." He gave a shrug of resignation. "Oh well, it's not as if there's anything worth watching on the telly tonight. What can go wrong?"

Glock continued. "We will begin by you telling me how Germany lost the war."

"I don't know exactly how you lost; I just know that you did." David said.

"Surely such a momentous episode in your history is taught to every child in your educational facilities?" Glock enquired. "You seemed very knowledgeable about certain facts a moment ago when you were talking to my colleague."

"No... not really. Schools only teach kids about old kings and queens and boring stuff from hundreds of years ago. They think knowing about crop rotation in the early seventeen hundreds, or the Holy Roman Empire is more important. You're more likely to learn about the French and Russian's getting their heads chopped off, than you are about the Second World War." David explained. "Most of that stuff I said earlier is what I've learned from university and what I remember from watching old war movies or documentary programmes on the Discovery Channel."

"Hmmm." Glock paused for a moment in thought before he continued. "Then you will go to a library...You do still have those in 2016, don't you?"

"Yeah, we have libraries. In fact, I have a part-time job in one." David replied proudly.

"Good, then you will go. You will read in the history section about decisive battles and you will tell me what happened. You will tell me about the strategies that won and the errors that lost. Concentrate on the pivotal campaigns. Give me the names of the Generals that were involved. How they used their tactics. Strategy David, is the key word here. Are you clear on my instructions?"

"Hang fire General. I'm no Professor, I'm only a second-year student. Anyway, it would be quicker if I just asked Google?" David said.

"Bah, Goebbels doesn't know a thing about military tactics. He is just a frustrated actor with a movie camera." Glock scoffed dismissively.

"Not Goebbels, Google. It's an Internet search engine."

"Inter...what?" Glock asked.

"Internet. It's a world-wide connection of computers."

"Are you sure you don't mean Goebbels?"

"Positive."

"I'm sorry, but you'll have to explain these new words of yours to me."

"Just think of all the libraries in the world, only displayed on a screen on your desk at home and you can access any information you want by using a keyboard."

Glock seemed confused. "Your language from the future is strange to me. Never mind, you will use your computing device and go to this...internet...and look up the answers I seek using...Goebbels."

"Google." David corrected. "And that's all sweet and everything, but I need money to do that. My access was cut last week."

"Why? Are the secret police monitoring your communications?" Glock enquired.

"Secret police! What, no? Pay-As-You-Go General. No pay...no go."

"Then pay your bills, David."

"That's easier said than done. I have no money left and my landlady is on my case for the rent. I'm sure she's going to bust my ass and throw me out on it." David said.

"Believe me young man if I was your landlady, I would be breaking your backside too. Have you no concept of managing your money in the future?"

"We may have won the war, General, but we had to pay dearly for it. Freedom isn't as free as you think." David complained.

Another pause, then.

"Very well. This is not insurmountable. We can provide you with the funds necessary to make your Pay-As-You-Go...go." Glock assured.

"One question, how are you going to get money to me from 1943?" David asked.

"Do you have a bank account?

"Well, yeah I do, but it's kinda overdrawn a bit."

"This news is not surprising to me. What is your account number?"

David reeled off his sort code and account number to Glock thinking. "If this really is a scam, they'll manage to get the square root of sod all from my account."

Glock finalised the session. "If I'm correct, the next time you access your account you should have more than enough to enable you to reinstate this Internet of yours. Once you have done this, I shall arrange it so we speak again." Glock must have disconnected the link from his end as there was a sudden surge and David was back in his room, his eyes back to normal again.

"What a rush!" David said to himself out loud. He stood up and gently tested his footing. He felt a little woozy, but it was no worse than the feeling he got after sinking a few beers. "I must be getting used to this now?"

The thought that someone was playing an elaborate prank on him crossed David's mind. This whole box thing was really quite impressive, he had to give them that. But who? Who did he know with the means and motive to go to such lengths to trick him on this scale? Perhaps his mates from the library were pulling his leg again? Like the time they told him to ring up the stores and ask for a bucket of steam. No, this was too contrived for those simpletons. Whoever had put this one together was a seasoned practical joker, for sure. "If this is a scam, it sure beats the hell out of the Nigerian Prince." He made a note to return to the shop and have it out with that eccentric shopkeeper later. But for now, he decided to play along. It wasn't as if he actually believed he was talking to a bunch of Nazis from 1943. I mean that's just crazy...isn't it?

David padded over to the spot on the floor where he found his coat. He lifted it up and patted down the pockets until he felt a familiar weight. He pulled out a battered looking leather wallet and flicked open the stud catch. The contents were sparse. A spent bus ticket. A crumpled receipt from the antiques shop and a debit card. David prized the card from the little slot. Tapping the card against his chin, David stood alone in his room lost in thought. After his moments reflection he sprang into action, swinging his coat over his shoulder and bounding out of the door. He raced along the landing, down the stairs and smack-bang into Mrs Reynolds.

"David!" She exclaimed in surprise as he barrelled past her.

"Sorry, Mrs R, no time to stop and chat, I have to go out, it's proper important."

"What about my rent"? She called after him. "That's proper important too."

David was out of the front door and halfway down the garden path. "If Herr Glock is telling the truth, you'll have your rent by tonight...and some."

"Who is Herr Glock?" She shouted with increasing volume; her hands placed on the top of her hips.

But David left her standing in the doorway with her mouth wide open, staring after him as he receded down the street. With a large smile he called back to her. "My mum always told me you'll catch flies if you go around with your mouth open Mrs R." With that parting comment, David was gone.

David stood in the ATM queue with his hands thrust deep in his pockets. The person in front of him seemed to be using every available feature the automated teller had to offer. Whilst he waited, his fingers touched the scrap of card he had found earlier. He pulled it out and inspected it again, only this time there was more of the card than he remembered.

Had it grown in his pocket? There was definitely more card and more writing. The once fractured words were now clearly visible;

'Reich Antiquities Est. 1947. Proprietor H. Meyer'. He turned it over to reveal a handwritten inscription in pencil.

'Use…poke…to…ben…ars…loo..side…chim.' The writing abruptly finished mid-sentence.

The person in front had finally concluded their banking business and had moved on. David took his place in front of the machine. He offered his bank card up to the waiting mouth of the card aperture, he stopped millimetres from the slot. His hand was shaking, a thin film of perspiration began to form on his upper lip. There was noise behind him as another shopper impatiently waited for David to finish his turn. Taking a gulp of air, David pushed his card into the slot and listened as the motors whirred into life. Small rubber wheels grabbed hold of the card, swallowing it into its mechanical belly. The display screen beeped, prompting

David to enter his security code. Each stab of the numerical pad was accompanied by an electronic howl.

David could feel the anxiety bubbling up inside from the pit of his stomach in anticipation of what he would find. Waves of nausea started to make him feel lightheaded. He navigated through the menu once again and selected the balance option. Each key press threatened to be the last before the bank decided that enough was enough and retained his card. But the machine continued to whirr, delivering its customary beeps until David's balance was finally displayed.

Your Account Balance is: £260,120 and 18 pence.

You may withdraw a maximum of £250.

What would you like to do?

David was frozen in place, staring at the screen with his mouth open. "Excuse me." Came the shrill voice of the impatient shopper standing behind David. "But are you going to be much longer, or are you catching flies with that mouth?" Eventually, with an almighty roar, David shouted at the ATM. "YOU NAZI SONS OF BITCHES!"

CHAPTER 6
LONDON, 2016

"So, you have received our modest donation, David?" Claus Glock enquired when they had reconnected the paranormal link.

"That depends on what you consider modest?" David spluttered. "But yes, thank you. Your deposit was very generous."

"I imagine 73 years of interest have helped your situation? Let us call it a work-related incentive. The first of many payments. But, young master David, we are not funding you for free now, after all. The money in your account will help you access this Internet device of yours. Depending on the information you give me, there is going to be more money for you...a lot more. I will make you a very rich man, young David."

David's thoughts kept returning to the balance displayed in little green digits on the ATM's screen. He'd never had that much money before in his life. The thought of that, and with the promise of more money to come, helped to anaesthetise the reality of what he was about to do. "Looks like history is about to pay out." He said.

Glock shifted the conversation up a level, his tone taking on an ominous inflection in David's inner mind. "Ask Goebbels everything about the period from June 1939 to the end of 1945." Glock's voice pervaded David's skull and cut across his little daydream, bringing him back to reality with a resounding, and somewhat sickening, blow.

"l want all the details you can find on any German defeats, specifically the Allied victories where we lost decisive ground. Dates, times, locations...l want the names of the Generals in charge of each skirmish, even the names of the chauffeurs that drove them. You are to leave nothing out. I give you until this time tomorrow, David." The link was severed and David returned to his reality.

The sound of a distant cuckoo clock roused him from the somnambulant state the box left him in when emerging from one of his sessions. He remained half-slumped in his chair, mindlessly counting out the birdie-chirpings that cut through the headache, which had taken up position in the front of his head. His brain was throbbing in time with the chimes. "…six, seven, eight, nine…Oh, crap! I'm late for work." He stumbled up and out of his door and staggered along the hallway. He descended the stairs one step at a time, clutching onto the bannister rail. He reached the bottom and squinted at the Swiss clock on the hallway wall, now past the hour it's little door tightly shut. Just the swinging oak leaf pendulum ticked by the remaining minutes until the next chorus of tweeting was due. David pressed a finger to his lips and shushed the clock. "Noisy!" He opened the front door and headed to the bus stop to catch the 9:20 into town. As the front door closed, so did Mrs Reynolds door, which David had failed to notice was left ajar. The landlady had watched him stumble past and drew her own conclusions.

"Drunk! At this hour. Disgraceful. He'll have to go."

David arrived at the library two hours late. With a beseeching look he held up his hands to the senior librarian in a conciliatory manner. "I'm so sorry, Judith." He whispered.

"David! Where have you been?" Judith questioned. "You look terrible, are you alright?"

David wanted to tell his work colleague everything that had happened, but when it came to articulating the events of the last 24 hours, he realised how fantastical it all sounded. No one in their right mind would believe him. He wasn't sure he believed it himself.

"Late one, sorry. Won't happen again." He said.

Judith gave him one of her, 'I care for you, but I don't approve' looks. "Well, you're here now, no one's been killed." She half joked. "Your lucky, Mr Granger is still in a meeting. He hasn't noticed you weren't in yet. Quickly, before he finishes there is still the Political Sciences section that needs reorganising from rows G to K, oh and can you please tidy up the Philosophy section. We had a group of rowdy philosophers in earlier who ransacked the shelves from Descartes to Nietzsche.

"Sure thing, Judith. I'll get right on it."

David set to work. It took all but thirty minutes to straighten out politics. By the time he'd tackled philosophy his headache had gone completely. He had the rest of the afternoon to get in some research of more recent historical events. By six o'clock Judith came looking for him.

"Hello David, it's closing time. Are you coming?" She asked as she walked across the foyer to the reference section.

David was engrossed in his research and barely noticed her standing over his shoulder.

"What you looking up?" She quizzed.

"Huh? Oh hi, sorry, I didn't hear you."

Judith saw the page David had open on the monitor. "Hitler? Why are you reading about him for?" She asked in a tone of disapproval.

"It's for my course work. I have a dissertation due in by tomorrow." David wasn't exactly telling fibs at this point. He just omitted to tell Judith who his new professor was. "You know what. I'm going to be a few more hours, so I'll stay on. Don't worry, I'll ask Charlie to lock up after me."

Judith smiled. "Well, alright. But don't leave it too late. We all know Charlie likes to get his head down before midnight. So much for a night watchman." Judith squeezed David's arm and left him scanning the internet.

David worked into the small hours referencing and cross referencing against all the historical facts Glock had asked for. The night watchman had stopped checking on him hours beforehand. By the time he finished, it was well past three in the morning. He covered a yawn with the back of his hand.

Turning off the monitor, he gathered his belongings and stood. Only after stretching out his stiff muscles did it dawn on him that he had not moved from that chair in fifteen hours, no wonder he was aching. He walked over to the closet room Charlie jokingly referred to as his office. The sounds of steady snoring reverberated from behind the door. David continued on by and let himself out by the side entrance. The door swung back on its gas strut and closed with a soft click, as the Yale latch locked it behind him. There were no buses running at this hour. He would have to walk home. He reckoned he'd make it just before sunrise.

David fell into his bedroom just as the first lick of the morning's light heralded a new day. There was a creak outside is room, the two shadows were back at the foot of his door.

"Doesn't that woman ever sleep?" He thought. "I'll square up with her later. First things first."

He sat down in front of the box, eager to impart all the knowledge he'd accumulated before his addled, sleep-starved brain shut down and forgot everything. David initiated the link and handed over the future to the NAZI's.

He relayed the information Glock had requested in magnificent detail. He started with how RADAR had played a key role in helping the British win The Battle of Britain, the air war waged from July to October 1940, between the Luftwaffe and the RAF. He told him that on July 9, 1941 their Enigma communications had been decrypted by Alun Turing's 'Ultra' team at Bletchley. This allowed the Allied forces to eavesdrop on Wehrmacht, Luftwaffe and Kriegsmarine orders. Soon after this the German Wolf-Packs, which had been waging unrestricted war on shipping since 1939, were hunted down and decimated.

December 7th 1941, Japan launched their surprise attack on the American fleet at anchor in Pearl Harbour, waking the sleeping dragon and bringing the might of the American armed forces into the Allied camp.

He explained how Hitler's meddling and ideological obsession in conquering the Ukraine, had deferred the army chiefs plans to invade Russia. This delay resulted in a woefully under-equipped conquering army faltering in the biting Russian winter. When the beleaguered 6th Army finally arrived at the gates of Stalingrad, they entered into brutal close quarters combat. After five months, one week and three days, the 6th Army finally ran out of food and ammunition. Despite specific orders by Hitler to fight to the last man, the German army surrendered, their fighting spirit crushed. History had recorded this as a decisive turning point in the war.

Each narration from the history texts detailed an ever more humiliating German defeat. Glock interrupted with indignant cries of..."impossible!" Followed with vitriolic tirades of abuse, directed predominantly at the senior officers, who in

Claus's view had been responsible for Germany losing the war. David got the impression that Glock seemed to know most of these people at a personal level. After today's history lesson, he didn't expect many of them would survive the night.

When David started to describe the events of June 6th 1944 and the incredible news of Operation Overlord, Glock was apoplectic with rage. The very thought of thousands of allied troops landing on the Normandy beaches and sweeping across occupied France, sent him into a hysterical fit. "Our defences were overrun because the Fuhrer was taking a nap and his aides were too afraid to wake him until midday?!" Glock ranted. "If this is true then Germany deserves to lose the war." He spat with barely concealed contempt.

"But you did lose it." David reminded him. "On the 8th May, 1945. Germany surrendered, unconditionally."

Glock remained silent; a dangerous brooding was evident in his irregular breathing. David continued to read from the pages of history, finishing with the events of Los Alamos and the Manhattan Project.

"The A-Bomb was destined to be dropped on Berlin." He said "But you lot stuck your hands in the air before it was ready. So they dropped it on Japan instead, twice."

"America split the atom first!?" Glock spluttered.

"Yup. One on August 6th and the other on the 9th 1945. The world's first and so far, only atomic detonations used as a result of war."

"This is incredible. But how did they manage to deliver the weapon?" Glock asked.

"Well, it wasn't by UPS, that's for sure, otherwise Japan would have woken up to a card on their doorstep saying… 'Sorry we missed you.'"

"Focus young man. This is not the time for levity." Glock chided. "Tell me how the Americans managed to transport this bomb over the target."

"They dropped them from a Boeing B-29 Superfortress bomber. One over a place called Hiroshima and the other called Nagasaki. The Japanese had no option but to surrender. Soon after, peace broke out and all hostilities across an exhausted planet ended."

"Tell me more about the power of this device." Glock effused.

"It's quite a sobering thought really. The first bomb instantly vaporise a city and killed up to 90,000 people in one go, with a further 50,000 succumbing to the effects of radiation poisoning in the following months."

"90,000 people in one go! Mein God, how big was it?"

"The bomb had an explosive yield of 15 kilotons of TNT"

"The largest ordinance we have is the 'Herman' and that is only one thousand kilograms." Glock did a quick mental sum. "Imagine what another one hundred and thirty thousand Herman's can do…all in one little bomb."

"The destructive power of the bomb was deemed so awful that no country has ever used one again. But ever since the first detonation at Trinity, the genie was let out of the bottle. We've been living under the threat of nuclear annihilation ever since."

The news of an atomic bomb sent Glock into a hysterical fit of pure excitement. He positively revelled at the prospect of getting hold of such a fantastic weapon, convinced that to do so was Germany's fundamental right as a superior race. It also proved that the rumours of a weapon that harnessed the power of a star were true. It was just a pity that the wrong side were going to get them first. The thought of a race of 'Untermensch' beating German scientists to such a glorious feat of supreme power, which by God's hand should rightfully be theirs, annoyed Glock the most.

It wasn't just David who had been keeping busy the past 24 hours. Von Riker had spent the night developing something he called a 'neural wave trans-matter compensator'. With this additional gizmo, he could intercept the neural energy exchange between the two operators, convert it and transcribe the brainwave patterns into an electronic format. All communications were now recorded on rotating magnetic tape spools and back-up copies printed out. As David diligently worked through the time line, Von Riker had been studying the concertina spools of printouts, furiously scribbling notes as the pages issued forth. A steady stream of runners ferried the documents to various departments, where it was disseminated and cogitated by strategists in minute detail. When von Riker saw the Manhattan transcript, he personally implemented a plan to correct this obvious imbalance.

With each day of history transmitted, a little more of David's external reality began to be stripped away. David's physical body was cocooned by the growing time vortex. The space he occupied had become isolated from the events going on around him. The box had a cushioning effect, shielding him from reality by an invisible protective bubble. Inside the vortex David was oblivious to anything. The world outside this bubble however, began to distort. His room had become supercharged with static electricity. Thick blue tendrils of lightening laced the air, caressing anything it connected to with a deadly touch of raw energy. Loose material started to spiral around the room, rising in intensity until all the contents of David's bedroom became a swirling maelstrom of light and matter. The air, heavy with the smell of ozone, crackled and fizzed with charged particles. The vortex pulsated with a menacing thrum; the circumference of its leading edge was surrounded by the pure black wall of a void. The singularity began growing ever outward, consuming all in its path. A frantic hammering noise came from the other side of the door as someone pounded the wood with their fists.

"What on earth is going on it there? You stop that noise right now and pack your bags. I've had enough. David, I'm evicting you. I don't care where you go, but you are not staying in my house another night. Do you hear me, young man?"

The flimsy bedroom door finally gave way to the gravitational forces from the time vortex and ripped off its hinges, where it joined the tornado of debris swirling around an ignorant figure, huddled over a box. Mrs Reynolds was exposed, her fist still raised in the air, mid pound. Her expression dissolved from anger and her eyes widened in fear at the sight of the energy ball, mere feet from her face. Before she could utter a single word, a raw finger of pure energy whipped across the void and lashed into her body. The unformed contortion of a strangulated cry died on her lips, as the corpulent form of her body was dragged by the vacuum into the time distortion and Mrs Reynolds winked out of existence, taking with her any back rent due. The explosion happened instantaneously. A nano second later the room and everything in it disappeared in a blinding white flash.

CHAPTER 7

A loud, but persistent rapping started to percolate through the fringes of David's consciousness. It brought him back from the depths of his time-trance. The ethereal link between David and the box began to crumble, letting the tide of reality come crashing down with a sucking pop! David was fully awake and back in a bedroom, although not quite his bedroom. He surveyed the room taking in the familiar items. Throughout the seemingly normal surroundings, there were subtle differences. The first being how clean his room was. The box was there, brooding on the table. The knocking persisted.

David got up from his chair to answer the door. Instinctively, he felt in his pocket for the thick wodge of cash he'd drawn from the ATM.

"Alright Mrs Reynolds." He said to the door. "I'm coming and I have your rent."

He pulled out the bundle of notes, ready to wave them smugly in her face, but failed to notice that the crisp, 'Tens' and 'Twenties,' that he had withdrawn from the ATM earlier in the day, had changed. Instead of the Queen's head adorning the currency, he was now waving a fist full of Reichsmarks instead.

He reached out for the handle, a wide grin planted squarely on his face and pulled back the door. His smile dissolved and was replaced by a cautious frown at the sight of two stern looking men greeting him instead of his landlady.

"Can I help you?" He asked, looking at their strange clothes.

"Herr Meyer?" The taller of the two men asked.

"That depends on who's asking." David replied, his brow creased tighter.

The man held up a sheet of paper bearing the photograph of David's face pinned to the top left corner. Large black letters spelled out the words; "ARREST WARRANT"

"You are Mr David Meyer?" The man persisted.

"I never said it wasn't. And you are?" David asked.

"You are to come with us." The man barked with authority. The tone of his voice meant that this was not a voluntary request.

The two men were wearing identical beige trench coats, the waists gathered together and held tight by a belt. Shiny brogues protruded from the ankles of pressed black trousers, the creases running down their centres looked like they were sharp enough to cut paper. The tops of their heads were covered with charcoal grey Trilbies and they both reeked of expensive cologne.

One of the men was checking the time against a silver pocket watch which bore the engraved inscription;

'To Herr Stöller
For 25 years' service to the Kriminalpolizei
A. Nebe'

"Nice watch." David observed.

"Thank you." The man said. "It was my father's".

A long chain disappeared into his overcoat, which was attached to a tailored waistcoat underneath. As he flipped the lid open it played a short piece of classical music; Wagner. David instinctively went to look at his own wrist. Damn it! He never got his watch fixed. Proffering his wrist to the pocket watch man, he asked for the time. The first of the two men stepped forward and grabbed hold of David's wrist, expertly slapping a pair of handcuffs on him in one, swiftly executed, movement.

The second man looped his arm through David's and together, all three of them marched along the landing. As they descended the stairs David saw Mrs Reynolds waiting at the bottom, but there was something different about her. She was as fat as ever, probably more than David had remembered and she was still wearing the billowing frock, but her hair was different. It was now a golden-blonde and pinned up in the large curled plaits of a Bavarian dairy maid. As David was led passed her, he managed to catch sight of something metallic pinned to her lapel. He couldn't be absolutely certain, but in his fleeting glimpse, David thought he saw a Swastika. He spun his head around to look at one of the men.

"That's not Mrs R." He jerked his shoulder and tried to duck under the Gestapo man. The handcuff pulled taught and a sudden pain in his wrist halted his attempts. "Hey, let go of me. Where are you taking me?" He demanded.

"Silence!" The tall man snapped, slapping David's face with the back of his free hand. He then turned his head and nodded his appreciation to Mrs Reynolds as they pushed David past her. "Thank you, Frau Reynolds. Your valuable information has proved very useful. Your dedication to the Party is greatly appreciated."

Mrs Reynolds smiled awkwardly whilst attempting to give her best curtsy. The cuckoo made a solitary appearance. It sounded for all the world to say; 'Goodbye'.

"I'd watch that one, if I were you. An idle, rudderless no-hoper if ever there was. Never pays his rent, mind." She spat at David as he was dragged away. With a look of smug satisfaction on her face she disappeared back into her living room. From behind a thin veil of net curtains hanging from the bay window, Mrs Reynolds watched David as he was manhandled down the path and bundled into the back of a dark grey BMW saloon.

Concealed behind heavily tinted windows, the unseen driver floored the accelerator, sending the car and its occupants screeching up the street in a cloud of choking smoke. No one noticed the two elderly gentlemen walking up behind. One quite tall, the other fat.

David was sandwiched between the two Gestapo men, as he watched the houses zip by in streaks of grey. The skyline had morphed into vast monolithic constructs, which loomed out of the ground like wizened concrete fingers reaching up to scrape the sky. The glass fronted office buildings and red brick dwellings of David's old world had been replaced with wall-to-wall concrete, in a stark statement that betrayed the national socialism of the architect's state of mind. Row after row of tower blocks jutted out of a drab sea of concrete, like an artist employing passionless brushstrokes to daub the countryside with featureless monochrome. Functionality dominated aesthetics. Unimaginative materials swallowed the raw soul of the buildings, which gave birth to the hidebound vision of the utilitarian's idea of national architecture. Familiar landmarks were no longer visible against the Capital's skyline, replaced instead by these alien structures of foreign origin, which led David to believe that he was no longer in England.

"What happened to London?" He asked his passengers.

"What do you mean, what happened to London?" The Gestapo officer replied. "It looks the same to me."

"But where have all the buildings gone? The Shard, Canary Warf, The London Eye?"

"Never heard of any of those before, what about you Lanz?" The man asked his colleague.

"No, never."

"Alright then, what about St Pauls, you've heard of that, right?" David persisted.

"St Pauls what?"

"The cathedral, you know? Big domed building. Hundreds of years old. Sir Christopher Wren. No! really? What about the Houses of Parliament, Big Ben? You must know those?"

The Gestapo man looked at David quizzically. "Ah…you're talking about all those old buildings that got destroyed in 43'?"

"Destroyed!" David cried.

"Yes, most of London has been rebuilt from the ground up after the war. There wasn't much left standing after the A-Bomb."

"A-Bomb! On London…No, no, no. That's not right. It was Japan they dropped the bomb on, not London."

"No, on May 17th 1943, London was the first city to be attacked using the German 'Fetter Junge' bomb. Two days later the Luftwaffe dropped the 'Dunner Mann' bomb on Moscow and Japan hit Washington D.C with their A-Bomb. That's how Germany and the Axis forces won the war."

"But it didn't happen like that. The Americans were the first to develop the bomb." David protested.

"The Americans! Ha, they were nowhere close to developing the bomb. The father of the atomic age was Werner Heisenberg's and his team, Operation Uranium."

"But that's not right!" David continued to object.

"Pipe down." The Gestapo man ordered. "Right or not, the history books don't lie." The Gestapo man turned once again to his colleague, jabbing his thumb in David's direction. "This one has been watching too many of those alternate reality films on the PKD channel." Both men laughed.

It is often said that history is written by the victors. Only this time it wasn't Churchill, Roosevelt or Stalin with the pen in their hands. The contemporary books of this reality had been crafted by Adolf Hitler, Benito Mussolini and Emperor Hirohito. History had played out very differently in this new reality.

The Soviet threat had been neutralised in the spring offensive of 1943 code named: Operation Barbarossa, in which the Wehrmacht essentially closed the eastern front. Originally scheduled for the summer of '41, military intelligence convinced Hitler to change his mind and postpone the offensive for two years. By missing the unseasonably wet summer of '41 and harsh Russian winters, the Germans were spared from fighting the elements as well as the Russians.

This also gave the German war machine extra time to build up the logistics needed in order to support the massively insane number of supplies and equipment, needed to penetrate deep into the Motherland. On April 5th, three Army groups spearheaded by General Guderian's Panzer Division, raced across the Steppes. Despite capturing many critical reserves, the vast distances and harsh conditions still managed to take its toll on the blitzkrieg. The initial momentum stalled after the six-week dash and the might of the Axis battlegroup ground to a halt on May 10th, twenty kilometres from Moscow. The Germans were met with fierce opposition from a stubborn foe, desperate to keep the grey wolf from the doors of the Capital. After a further nine days of siege fighting, Goering dropped the Dunner Mann bomb on Moscow and the Bolshevik menace was consumed in Hell's Inferno. Hitler was now free to concentrate his forces on a single, western front.

On 20th May 1943, the Luftwaffe used a Heinkel HE 177 long range heavy bomber, to deployed the 'Fetter Junge' bomb on London. Three weeks later the Nazi's finally launched 'Operation Sea Lion'. The invasion of Great Britain. Hitler's 9th and 16th Army landed shock-troops from Brighton to Dover beach, while airborne Fallschirmjäger paratroopers were dropped all over the Kent countryside. A second wave of mechanised troops, including seven panzer divisions under the command of Generaloberst von Rundstedt, landed at Portsmouth in amphibious assault crafts. The advancing might of the Wehrmacht, made up from thousands of battle-hardened soldiers, swept through the tissue-paper thin resistance offered up by the LDV force and neutralised any remaining English defences in standard Blitzkrieg fashion. The country had no soldiers left to offer up in defence of the sovereign soil, after The British Expeditionary Forces were cut off at Dunkirk and captured. In this timeline, Hitler did not issue his 'Stop Order' and the

Germans got to the beaches before the little boats could manage the crossing.

Another victory came by employing RADAR, a new German invented technology, which allowed the Luftwaffe to decimate the fighting capabilities of the RAF, leaving the skies free for the military might of the invasion force to sweep up-country and take the capital in only two and a half weeks. Most of the Royal Navy's fleet were at the bottom of the English Channel, leaving Raeder's Kriegsmarine and Doenitz's Wolf Packs supremacy of the sea. This was partly in thanks to the newly re-engineered Enigma code machine, which British Intelligence had failed to crack.

The country, already reeling from the devastation of the atomic explosion, was caught off guard by the tenacity of the 'Red-Eyed Soldiers', which seemed immune to the effects of radiation. British Generals were astounded by the lightning speed and Teutonic efficiency the Germans had used to conduct their victory. Britain capitulated 24 hours before the first jackboot walked through the door of Number 10. Two days later, Churchill's government signed the British Instrument of Surrender in front of Generaloberst Alfred Jodl.

Churchill and his entire cabinet were tried as war criminals. They were executed on the steps of the Old Bailey. Those senior officials who survived the invasion, languished in tiny stone cells on Dartmoor, waiting to discover what fate lay in store for them. The most bizarre aspect of the assault, which continued to keep the British generals guessing, was how in the hell the Germans seemed to be one step ahead of them all the time!

The BMW continued to weave its way through the unfamiliar streets. The closer to the capital they got the more militarised it became. Sentry huts fortified with sandbags and razor wire slowed their progress. The car swerved as the driver negotiated his way around the concrete roadblocks. Each sentry hut had a queue of stationary traffic snaking behind it, adding to the congestion. David watched as the armed Feldgendarmerie guards performed roadside checks on all vehicles entering and leaving the Capital. Their highly polished metal crescents dangled from thick chains around their necks, dazzling in the reflective sunlight. Slung across their heavy ankle-length greatcoats was the standard army issue Schmeisser MP60 machine-pistol. A much-improved version of its MP40 cousin.

The BMW displayed a special set of plates which the uniformed guards recognised and quickly waved it through with a hasty salute. David noticed that each sentry station was assigned a Kripo agent, working alongside the uniformed guards. The sight of this turned David's thoughts to where he was being taken...and what was waiting for him when he got there?

He didn't have to wait much longer. The car pulled into a wide avenue which David instantly recognised as The Mall, although, now it had been renamed to; Victory Strasse. The long red asphalt surface was lined either side by impressive Doric columns each adorned by a 20-foot swastika banner and perched atop sat a lofty Party eagle. The regal stone creatures had the appearance of looking down their noses at the citizens, in a statement of arrogant disdain. The BMW continued down the Avenue at a sedate pace, its tyres crunching on the road surface as it passed.

The sky was suddenly obscured by a curtain of darkness cast from the passing shadow of a 150ft Zeppelin, as it cut across the road dwarfing the saloon and plunging the occupants into an artificial eclipse. The driver flicked on the headlamps and then flicked two fingers at the Zeppelin. He issued a gruff curse to the officers and crew of the floating leviathan. They didn't hear him. The drone from the dirigible's three fan-bladed propellers vibrated the air with a throbbing hum, as it clawed through the sky with inexorable effort towards the airship landing port at Croydon Aerodrome.

As the Zeppelin lumbered away another sight was revealed through the front windscreen. David could see an impressive regal building peeking out at the far end from behind a large memorial fountain, its Portland stone facade just beginning to push through the sparse foliage of the early spring trees. It was one of the most widely known and instantly recognisable buildings in the world and now it awaited his arrival. Home to the former residence of Great Britain's Royal family, who were in permanent hiding in South America, Buckingham Palace was now the combined home to the Deutschland Strategic Occupying and Civil Obedience Forces and the operational headquarters of the Geheime Staatspolizei. The incumbent commandant and supreme commander of the British Reich was currently fulfilled by one of the grandchildren of Heinrich Himmler, SS Oberst Gruppenfuehrer Vossmeister.

The domineering flagpole mounted high on the palace roof still reached up into the London sky, however, the Royal Standard had not flown over the roof of the palace in seventy years. Instead, adorning the historic frontage either side of the famous balcony, were two enormous red banners which undulated in the gentle breeze, a giant black Swastika announcing to the world whom the new residents were. Much of the palace had been largely destroyed in the NAZI A-Bomb blast, but such was Albert Speer's love for the architecture of the building that he personally oversaw its re-build. Once renovations had been completed in 1954, the palace was officially designated as the UK Reichstag.

David was being escorted deep into the heart of the sinister looking building. The last thing he heard before the great doors closed behind him was...

"Welcome to Gestapo Headquarters Herr Meyer.'

CHAPTER 8

THE UK REICHSTAG: GESTAPO DIVISIONAL HQ

BUCKINGHAM PALACE, 2016

David could not tell how long he had been left alone in the featureless room. It was obvious at first glance that the room he had been thrown into had never been intended for important palace business. His wrists and ankles had been tied to an old tubular framed chair, minus its seat pad. 'What's the point in keeping a broken chair about the place and why am I tied to it?' He thought. His feet were cold. He glanced down and saw his bare feet were touching the uncarpeted floor.

"What are they keeping me locked up for?"

He was sure it had been hours, but without his watch he had no way of telling. Come to think about it, with his watch he had no way of telling. It was one of the last things that the Gestapo had removed from him upon his arrival. A large meat-fisted Inspector had stuffed it into a thick paper bag, along with the rest of his clothes and possessions when he was ordered to strip. He winced at the memory of how thorough his captors were and at what lengths they would go to, to ensure he wasn't concealing anything. Only after they were satisfied and they had washed their hands, did they hand him a pair of disposable overalls to wear. The desk officer then catalogued David's items, scrawling a note in the margins of his paperwork. 'One wristwatch. Make German. Broken.'

The noise of keys jangling from the other side of the door broke his reverie. The lock turned and the door swung open allowing a senior looking officer, accompanied by a guard to enter the room. The guard took up position behind the officer and pointed a rifle at David. The officer circled David once. He inspected each of the binds that were keeping David secured to the chair.

David looked at the officer. He wore a black SS uniform tailored to project authority and foster fear. On each of his collar tips were the silver oak leaves and three diamond pips indicating the rank and insignia of Oberst-Gruppenfuehrer. His highly polished boots clicked against the hard floor. He wore a wrist band on his left sleeve featuring the motto; 'Meine Ehre heißt Treue' (My Honour Is Loyalty). He stood 6ft 3inches tall with a jutting chin and chiselled features. Below the peak of his hat was a battle-worn face sporting a jagged pink scar which ran from just below his left eye, scything along his cheekbone and trailed off down his neck, disappearing below his shirt collar. The wound pulled down his eyelid revealing more of the eyeball than was comfortable to look at. The officer leaned in closer to David. David could smell stale coffee on his breath, he recoiled at both the smell and the sight of the man. The officer continued to lean forward until the tip of his nose was touching David's nose. He drew in a sharp breath.

"Have a good look at it." He spoke. David turned his head in disgust. The officer grabbed David by the chin and forced his head back.

David watched as the unnaturally large eyeball rotated in the fleshy socket of the officer's head. The piercing green iris and pinpoint pupil almost seemed to lick David's face.

The officer let go of David's chin and straightened. He pulled down his tunic and plucked a gold-framed monocle from his breast pocket. Retrieving a pressed handkerchief from his trouser pocket, he polished the lens of the eyepiece and inserted it under his eyebrow.

"A souvenir from one of your friends."

"My Friends?" David responded, not understanding what the officer meant.

"A little surprise package planted by the British resistance under my staff car a year ago. Intended, no doubt, to aid in the removal of my presence in office. As you can see, the attack failed and fifty of your friends were rounded up and shot in reprisal."

"Resistance? A bomb! I don't know what you're talking about. That has nothing to do with me. I don't know anyone like that."

The officer let out a guttural laugh. "Perhaps not yet, but there is still time."

"I'm sorry?" David spluttered, "I don't understand. You have it all wrong. Everything is VERY WRONG."

"Acht, but of course. You are an innocent bystander, caught up in all," he paused," this." The officer punctuated his sentence by swirling his hand around in the air. "But what is…this, huh, this…what? You can perhaps tell me what…. this is….yes?"

"I don't know what you mean. I don't know who you are?"

"It would seem that I have you at a disadvantage. Very well, allow me to introduce myself. I am SS-Oberst-

Gruppenfuehrer Vossmeister. Pleased to meet you. I am the Supreme Commander of the British Reich. Now, you know who I am…David…Yes, no need for you to introduce yourself. I already know who you are. But listen to me, I'm talking too much. It is you whom should be doing the talking, pray continue with your explanation."

"I was at home and something happened. My landlady, who isn't my landlady will tell you. I haven't done anything wrong. But something is definitely wrong." David mewled.

"Oh, you mean Mrs Reynolds?" Vossmeister assured.

"Yes, Mrs Reynolds. Only she's not Mrs Reynolds, though. Not to me, anyway."

"No! Then who is she, if she's not Mrs Reynolds?"

"I don't know. I mean, she looks like Mrs Reynolds, only different. And out there, the streets and city. They're all wrong."

"Perhaps, it is you who is wrong, David? Have you thought about that?"

"Me! I don't understand what is happening, but the one thing I'm certain of is that I'm the only thing about all this that is real." David was at the point of sobbing.

"There, there young David. You are getting yourself all worked up. Try and relax, here let me loosen your binds. I don't think we need these anymore, do you?" The guard sharpened the aim of his rifle as Vossmeister untied David's hands and feet.

"There, that's better. However, I think you are right about one thing though, when you say that you are the only one who is real."

"Thanks." David managed, as he massaged his wrists and ankles. "What do you mean?" He asked.

"David, let me assure you the one thing Germans are very good at, is keeping records. We hold accurate records of every single person living in this country…except for one…You. We have no record of you…at all. One minute you don't exist and, all of a sudden, overnight if you will, 'poof' there you are, as real as you are sitting in front of me now. Absurd as it sounds, it's almost as if you just 'popped' into existence. You are an anomaly and the one thing I don't like is anomalies, David. The other thing that is real is the sudden interest Berlin has in you. Why would that be, I wonder?"

"Well, if you don't know, then what chance do I have?"

"Let me tell you what I do know, shall I?" Vossmeister crouched down, his damaged eye fixed on David, unblinking. "Two days ago, I received orders from the Reichsmashall himself. These orders specifically stated that you were to be apprehended and detained ahead of those interested parties arriving from Berlin I mentioned a moment ago. I find myself asking the question, why have these people become very interested in YOU, David. To me this is very strange, is it not?"

"Strange?" David coughed. "You think that's strange? You want to be where I am, then you'll know, strange."

"The people who are coming to see you David are not as good natured as I. If, however, you could tell me where you came from, how you got into the country, then perhaps I could make things go a bit smoother for you."

"But I told you, I don't know anything. And what do you mean where did I come from? I come from West Acton and I have always lived in this country. I was born in Hammersmith."

Vossmeister stood, his uniform creaked in protest as the leathers stretched. "Very well. If you persist in playing your little 'Mr Innocent me' game, then I cannot help you." He turned to leave.

"Wait!" Cried David, leaping to his feet. The guard sprang into action, stepping forward and halting David's advance with the muzzle of his rifle. He pressed it into David's chest. "What's going to happen to me? These people what do they want from me? Is it about the money?"

Vossmeister stopped and turned back to face David. He let out a genuine sigh of remorse before answering. "I wish I knew the answer to that. These people do not broadcast their intentions to anyone. Not even me, David and I am the most senior person there is in England. The fact that you seem to have over two hundred thousand Reichsmarks in your account is not inconsequential, but not of concern to these people. They are not interested in money. You will most probably be taken to one of their 'Black Sites' where you will be interrogated and that will be the last the world ever sees of you, David. Unless you begin to tell me what I want to know."

David's head hung down to his chest. "But I don't know anything. It's all changed. My whole life has changed since I used that box. I don't belong here…I don't belong now."

"Box?" Vossmeister looked up with interest. "What box?" He enquired.

"The box I bought from the old antiques shop on the high street. Ever since I used it, that's when things started to change."

"Where is this box, now?" Vossmeister pressed.

"Dunno. At home still, I guess. In my room."

"Finally, we are getting somewhere. Thank you, David. I have to go now, but I will return. Stay here." Vossmeister spun around on his heels and walked through the door. The guard released his rifle from David's chest and followed close behind. The door swung shut and David heard the bolt being drawn back again. He was left alone in the room.

David shivered, he wrapped his arms tight around him in an effort to keep warm. He walked over to the door and tried the handle. Unsurprisingly, he found the door was locked. The room was small and unheated, despite an ornate fireplace set into the wall. There were signs that the fireplace had once been used, probably during the time when the original occupiers of the palace were still in residence. Now, the only thing that it was used for was to funnel a shrill wind down the chimney, where it fanned out into the room in an icy blast.

Looking out through the barred window, he discovered that his room was on the second floor of the building. From his limited view, he saw what would have been Horse Guards Parade. Instead of the Queen trooping the Colour, it was used to park a detachment of Panzers assigned to protect the UK Reichstag and its new occupants. He gripped the bars and gave them a testing shove; half hoping that he could somehow shake them loose. The bars remained a solid testament to the worker whom had installed them. David's shoulders dropped in resignation. It was hopeless to think he could escape the clutches of the Secret Police if he couldn't even manage to get out of a small, locked room.

David's heart jumped into his mouth as the door swung open again, this time it was the growling face of the Inspector who'd taken David's possessions filling the doorframe. In his giant-sized fist he held a paper sack. He tossed the bag in David's direction with a derisive snort.

"Get dressed." The Inspector spat through snarled lips at him.

The bag landed with a soft plop at David's feet. Another figure was lurking just out of sight behind the inspector.

"My pardon Inspector." The concealed voice said. The inspector didn't move, but displayed a look of irritation that betrayed his contempt at the interruption. "What do you want, worm?" He growled. The voice continued.

"Herr Vossmeister wishes you to give this to the prisoner." Now the inspector turned, partially revealing the hidden man who David noticed was quite fat. The man handed over a plate, which the inspector took. The man bowed and turned around, disappearing from sight. On the plate was a sticky bun, with a glistening icing sugar topping. The inspector picked up the bun and examined it. He brought it up under his nose and sniffed it. Then he stuck out an abnormally swollen tongue and scooped off the icing sugar in one large lick. He gave David a sadistic smile and threw the spoiled confection to the floor and the door slammed shut, the lock once again scraping back into the frame.

David ignored the licked bun, instead picking up the bag and peered inside. Gratefully, he pulled out his clothes and started to dress himself, pleased to see that his coat was still there. Whatever was going to happen to him, at least he'd be warm now. He retrieved his watch and automatically strapped it around his wrist. It never told the right time. He looked at the dial anyway; 22:01. "Figures." He thought.

His hands sought out the warm confines of his coat pockets where he found the impossible business card again. He pulled it out and inspected it for more information. The card was now fully restored and David gasped as he watched the jumble of words rearrange themselves in front of his own eyes. One by one they formed into a legible sentence.

"Use the poker hidden inside the fireplace to loosen the bars. Climb out of the window. Get yourself home and use the box again. Tell Glock to look at the Major, then destroy the box."

David stood for a moment with the card trembling in his hand. He looked over at the fireplace and back at the card, his brain slowly joining the dots between what the message was telling him and what his eyes were looking at. Then, with a sudden realisation the connection was made and David burst into action, making straight for the sooty opening of the fireplace. He skidded to his knees and peered up the flue and to his utter astonishment he saw a heavy iron poker nestling on a narrow ledge just inside the chimney, exactly as the card had said. David raced across the room and checked the door again. He listened for a minute before running back to the fireplace. Carefully, he lifted down the poker and walked over to the window. He paused for a moment whilst deciding where the best place to start was. He found a point above one of the brackets and inserted the poker and with all his weight, he leaned against the makeshift lever. The plaster cracked and discharged a few fragments onto the floor, but the reinforced bars continued to defy David's puny strength and remained stubbornly tight. The poker was too short, David needed something longer to give him more leverage.

He scanned the room, his eyes coming to rest on the broken chair with its missing seat pad. Bingo! Now he understood why the chair had been left there. The tubular design was a perfect fit over the poker's handle. David reinserted the poker between the bars. This time when he leant against it, the bars shifted slightly. It took a few more attempts before the wall mounted brackets were loose enough to be prized away from the shattered plaster and masonry. David eased the bars out of the frame as gently as he could and lowered them onto the floor, panting as he strained under their weight. He managed to walk the ironwork over to the door and jammed it under the handle. "My key's bigger than yours", he muttered, satisfied that the door was now secure. He returned to the debarred window and discovered the sash lock had been left open. Whoever had been in charge of security that day must have considered that the bars alone were enough to prevent entry to the room. Nothing had been put in place to cater for the other way round. David was not about to hang around and discuss the merits of this decision with himself.

He managed to lift up the window and climb out onto a broad stone ledge which ran along the length of the building's facade. David stood as thinly as he could, squashing his body flat against the stonework with his palms pressed inwards in a vain attempt to provide some imaginary suction. The room his captors locked him in wasn't far from the centre of the palace. Below him there was a drop of approximately thirty feet to the ground. With no intention of jumping from the ledge, he looked along the length of the building to see if there were any drainpipes, or service cables that he could use to slide down, but saw only the clean lines of mock Georgian architecture leading away either side of him. He set off to the right, in the hope that there would be something he could use around the corner of the building. The gusts of wind that had been whistling down the chimney were now buffeting his body, tugging at him and threatening to blow him off the ledge. As he rounded the corner, he saw the gigantic Swastika banners that adorned either side of the erstwhile Royal balcony, the wind ruffling the stiff fabric. David continued to inch along the ledge towards the balcony using sideways steps, his palms never leaving the surface of the stones.

Directly below the balcony a thoughtful tank commander had decided to park three of his Panzers. Instead of the Queens Guard in their bearskin Busbys, the UK Reichstag was protected by these metal monsters. David decided this was going to be his way down. He closed the gap with slow, determined paces, until he was within reach of one of the gigantic banners.

The Panzer Commander was standing up in the turret. He was barking into a pair of headphones. "Don't look up now." David urged. The growling purr of the Panzer's two Daimler gas turbine engines were turning over beneath his feet, sending up hot spouts of acrid exhaust fumes into David's face. The noise of the engines alone would prevent anyone from hearing his descent. He reached out and grabbed a fistful of red fabric in each hand and dangled his legs over the side of the ledge. Another powerful gust of wind whipped up the side of the building, spinning David around in mid-air. He gripped the cloth tight and waited for the oscillations to abate before continuing to abseil down. He inched his way toward the stationary tank.

When he was within a few feet from the rear of the Panzer the gentle purring of the idling engines erupted into a shrieking whine. The twin turbines revved up into their higher registers as the driver of the 40-tonne beast, dropped it into gear and floored the accelerator. David reacted instinctively and let go of the banner, dropping the final few feet onto the back of the tank. His feet hit the metal plating with almost no sound. He immediately flattened himself against the armour, frantically holding on by his fingertips in a desperate attempt to stop himself from being flung into the path of the tracks and crushed into a bloody pulp. David's miniscule weight failed to register against the steel goliath and the oblivious commander and his crew, hadn't noticed they'd picked up an extra passenger.

The Panzer lurched forward and rolled across the courtyard, heading toward a maintenance shed. Its road tracks had been fitted with rubber pads to prevent the tarmac from being chewed up. This did little to quieten the incessant squeaking that came from the revolving metal links. Combined with the roar of the turbines and the maddening vibrations, David thought that his head was about to explode. The driver threw the levers to negotiate a sharp corner and sent the tank slewing to the left. David's tentative handgrip disappeared and the momentum rolled him off the back, where he travelled through the air for the short distance it took gravity to bring him down to earth with a bone crunching thump. The Panzer rolled on, ignorant to any of this.

David scrambled to his feet, performing a quick pat-down to confirm that he still had all his limbs attached. The tank had disgorged him by an unmanned side gate, which David scaled without thinking to check whether it was locked or not. The adrenalin was pumping around David's body so hard that rational thinking became a by-product for his survival. He didn't notice the razor wire that was coiled along the top of the fence lacerate his clothing, slicing the fabric into tattered ribbons. Now on the other side of the fence, he allowed himself a quick glance over his shoulder. From behind one of the top storey windows David saw the silhouette form of a figure waving him on. It was difficult to tell from this distance, but it looked like a fat old man.

Free from the confines of the UK Reichstag, there was now the matter of getting back to his digs without being recaptured. He needed to make his way across London whilst evading a well organised army. He remembered how many checkpoints they had driven through on the way in. Main highways and thoroughfares were best to be avoided if he didn't want to be spotted. He'd have to keep to the side roads and alleyways and avoid contact with anyone. He was a person of extreme interest to the authorities and a stranger in his own country, he could trust no one.

He had no money for public transport, but that would be too risky anyway. The first thing the Gestapo would do would be to distribute his likeness to the armed squads that were stationed at all transport hubs. Or shoot him on sight. He needed to dump his coat and change his clothes. His opportunity came whilst passing the rear of the houses in one of the side roads. Many of the gardens had washing hanging out in them, which made it easy for a nimble-fingered fugitive on the run from the Gestapo, to procure a new shirt and trousers. He left a pile of ripped rags in exchange for his new wardrobe.

CHAPTER 9

It took the best part of the day for David to make his way across the city and back to West Acton. He had kept to the side streets and back alleys for most of his way, ducking the numerous sentry posts he'd seen on his way in. The London streets were gridlocked, the traffic backing up from Piccadilly Circus to Ealing Common. The Gestapo had cordoned off the Capital and thrown up roadblocks at every major junction, which made his progress fraught with danger. Helicopters circled above, officers from three counties scouted the streets with barking dogs straining at their chains. There were a hundred pairs of alerted eyes looking for him.

He arrived at his street a few moments before the sun set. The street lamps had started to flicker on, casting their yellow sodium glow. He paused at the top of the road, using the leaves of a shrubby garden to take cover. From his concealed position he scanned the rows of houses, looking for anything out of the ordinary. He checked to see if there were any cars that didn't belong parked in the street, or a twitch of the curtains from top floor windows. Everything looked normal. But, what was normal? The city streets and leafy suburbs of the nation's capital should not normally be swarming with Death's Head Stormtroopers.

After ten more minutes the sun had dropped below the suburban rooftops, David decided it was safe to chance it. He broke cover from the large and rangy rhododendron bush that had been providing his shelter, and ducked down the alleyway that provided access to the garages. The rear of the properties afforded plenty of protection from overlookers as the back gardens were enclosed by 6ft brick walls with solid wooden gates. He kept to the shadows and crouched along the narrow service road. He made it to his garden gate and with the precision of a bomb-disposal expert, he slowly lifted the latch, trying not to make a noise. "Don't you be locked!" he hissed. Pressing his shoulder to the gate he gave a shove. The gate eased open without a squeak. Once he was inside his back garden, he closed the gate and ensured the bolts were across. So far, so good. With the exception of the odd dog barking in the distance, no one had been alerted to his presence. David moved like a thief in the night down the garden path and pressed himself flat against the kitchen wall. The roof of the conservatory provided him with an easy way to reach the drainpipe that ran parallel with his bedroom window. With the agility of a cat, David scaled the wall and reached out for the sash window. He knew it would be left open, even during the depths of winter he never locked it.

His day hadn't finished handing out surprises, because as he pried the casement with his fingers, he found to his frustration it wouldn't budge. He was now exposed to anyone who happened to walk past, there was nothing else for it. He swung at the window with his elbow and winced as the pane of glass shattered into a hundred fragments. Shards of glass rained down onto the conservatory roof below in tinkling splinters. Without waiting to see if anyone had heard, he twisted the catch and lifted the window up, slithering in through the open gap and collapsed in a heap on his bedroom floor.

As David lay panting on his carpet, outside the front of the house, two grey Opel army trucks pulled up in a cloud of diesel smoke. The tailgates swung down in unison, issuing forth a platoon of well-trained stormtroopers, clutching Carbine rifles and Machine Pistols. In well-rehearsed fashion, they fanned out to form a wide semi-circular arc, the front row dropping to their knees, while the rear ranks gave cover from behind. They trained their weapons on David's house. Another truck skidded to a halt at the other end of the street, blocking off all access in and out.

The soldiers from the second truck moved out quickly to cover the back of the house. Their polished hobnailed boots indiscriminately trampled over the manicured gardens and crunched across the gravel and tarmac in military unison. The soldiers took up their positions and encircled the house in less than two minutes. An uneasy silence descended over the street, punctuated by the occasional rustle of combat fatigues and the faint clinking of metal, as rifle straps were adjusted in the hands of the soldiers. Only the subdued coughs betrayed the soldier's presence as they waited with their collective fingers poised over the trigger-guards. One of the trucks belched into life and lurched backward, opening up enough of a gap to let in a Daimler-Benz G8 staff car.

The car swept up the street and glided to a halt outside David's house. The driver disgorged himself and hurriedly opened the rear door, allowing the officer dressed in a black SS uniform to emerge and look up and down the street, checking the positions of the soldiers. He withdrew his Luger service pistol from its holster, drawing back on the cocking mechanism with one hand and reaching for a bullhorn that had been lying on the back seat with the other. He placed the microphone to his mouth and spoke.

"Good evening Herr Meyer. This is Oberst-Gruppenfuehrer Vossmeister. You remember who I am?" Vossmeister waited for a few moments. "I know you came home to use your box, so now you can use it. I must admit, you are more clever than my men. They could not find it. If you are thinking of making a break for it, I can assure you David, you cannot run. I hate to use such tired old cliches, but you are completely surrounded. You have precisely three minutes to surrender yourself. The alternative will not be very pleasant for you." The bullhorn squealed in final protest to Vossmeister's demand.

David sat up from where he had landed and looked around. His bedroom door hung off its hinges, the doorframe splintered where it had been kicked open. His room had been completely ransacked. Furniture had been turned over and smashed, the contents of his drawers ripped into rags and left strewn over the floor. His bed had been upturned and propped against the wall. A gaping hole had been left from the bayonet that had been used to eviscerate his mattress, it's stuffing left piled up in a discarded heap. Photographs lay on the floor in smashed frames, the glass ground to dust beneath the unforgiving heel of a boot. Even wide strips of wallpaper had been torn from the walls. David scrambled to his feet and began tearing at the debris of his room.

"No…No…No…It has to be here." He sobbed.

"David!" Came a shrill cry from the broken doorway. He spun round to see Mrs Reynolds beckoning him. "Hurry, we don't have much time. Quickly now, follow me." David stepped over the detritus and joined Mrs Reynolds. They hurried along the landing and stopped outside the bathroom.

"Mrs R, I'd just like to say this wasn't me, I didn't do that to my room."

"I know." She reassured him. "Two goons from the police turned up this morning. They were most insistent." She said whilst retrieving the key to the bathroom door from a chain around her neck and opening it. She looked at David. "Inside, come on…chop-chop."

They both entered the bathroom, David stopped and looked around as Mrs Reynolds walked straight over to the bath.

"Help me with this will you." She said as she began to loosen the bath panel. David grabbed hold of the other end of the panel and together they prized it open. In the recess beneath the enamelled tub was the box, wrapped up in an old blanket.

"Mrs R, you ledge…you hid it from them!" David exclaimed in barely concealed joy. "But I thought you were one of them? You turned me in."

"When the Gestapo turn up at your door it is not wise to openly defy them." She nodded to David and winked.

"But I've seen how these people operate." David said. "They don't miss anything; how did you manage to hide it from them?"

"Like all blunt instruments they use fear and intimidation to bully information out of you. But all the time they are raging, the calm mind can slip in the odd bit of subterfuge. Small enough so as not to notice. Soon after you were taken away, I had a visit from two gentlemen, claiming to be friends of yours. A nice pair, they said they owned that antique shop on the high street. They told me not to worry about you and that you'd be back. They also told me all about this box, and what it does. The fat one also ate all of my biscuits. They knew the shop was being watched though, so it wasn't safe to take it back there. They told me to hide it well. They were right about when the policemen would turn up too. Right down to the second."

"But if the Germans find out you've helped me, you'll be arrested. They'll probably kill you."

Mrs Reynolds grabbed David by the shoulders. Her soft eyes looked beseechingly into his as a single tear rolled down her ruddy cheek. "The only thing necessary for evil to triumph is for good men to do nothing. Edmund Burke said that 300 years ago."

From outside came the screech of the bullhorn again. "I am a patient man David, but today not so much. If you do not surrender now, I will be forced to come in and get you."

Mrs Reynolds took hold of David's arm, squeezing it tight. "David, I don't belong in this time, none of us do, especially them." She indicated to the street outside with a nod of her head. "I miss my Bert, take the box and bring me back to him. Now you must go, hurry. That Krout commander won't wait much longer." She helped David up and thrust the box into his arms.

Thanks to Oberst-Gruppenfuehrer Vossmeister's obsessional need to constantly inform his cornered prey about the passage of time, David knew he had only minutes before jackboots would be kicking down the door and a hundred soldiers would be goose-stepping their way up the stairs.

David wasted no time. "I need something flat to put the box on." He said.

"There, use this." Mrs Reynolds indicated to the bath panel. Together they raised it up and placed it over the bath. David grabbed a side table, tipping the array of shampoos and soaps onto the floor. He removed the box from the blanket, placing it on top of the panel and used the table as a stool. The planchette jumped into his hand and David made the last paranormal connection of his life.

Chapter 10

WEWELSBURG CASTLE—1943

SS PARANORMAL DIVISION

A dense mist shrouded the trees and houses in the fields below the castle. Elevated atop of the Alme Valley, the grey stone walls of the castle reflected the morning sunlight, giving the appearance as if the medieval structure was held aloft by the hand of a god. The mist hung in stubborn defiance, the opaque vapour suspended in an impermeable blanket, suffocating the surrounding hillside and cutting off the castle from the outside world.

The 14th century renaissance castle had a triangular layout, with three round towers connected by massive walls. For the past ten years it had been used as a school dedicated to the racial teachings of National Socialism. As the party's fortunes rose and his status along with it, Heinrich Himmler purchased the structure outright and expanded it into a complex referred to as; 'The Centre of the World.' The castle was now home to an SS cult of fanatical senior party members who called themselves; 'The Order'. They had made the castle their base of operations and used it to practice the occultist teachings of demonic metaphysical science, espoused by the Thule and Vril societies. This small group of dedicated Black Sun worshipers had become structured and highly organised under the occult obsessed Reichmarshall's leadership.

In the last year, he had invested a large portion of his own personal wealth into refurbishing the old medieval elements of the castle. The interior was furnished with miscellaneous objects of art and works by contemporary sculptors and painters in line with the aesthetics of National Socialism. Himmler's ultimate goal, together with the sympathetic cults, was to create new myths and turn it into a 'Grail Castle' once the Nazi's had established themselves as the new rulers of the world.

Stories of supernatural rites and dark magic practices performed by mysterious cloaked figures, were told by witnesses frequenting the local inns and taverns. An element of fear and superstition kept the locals from prying too much into the affairs of the castle. Often strange illuminations emanated at night, emitting an unearthly glow from within the walls and projecting ribbons of spectral light high into the sky.

A frenetic energy coursed through the castle as the day shift started their morning routine. Convoys of canvas covered trucks, book-ended by armoured escorts, thundered over the north moat bridge and disappeared under the substantial gateway, delivering their secret cargo deep into the beating heart of the castle. The sound of heavy machinery pervaded the stillness of the morning as diesel generators coughed into life, belching their noxious fumes into the air where it joined with the mist, fortifying the mix. Another noise joined the cacophony of whining turbines. An extra-terrestrial noise.

Fifteen years earlier, the NAZI's learned about a crashed disc-shaped object in the Black Forest near Freiburg. Under strict security the wreckage had been removed to the castle, where members of the Thule and Vril Societies, with assistance of the SS Technical Branch, now combined into Himmler's PSD, had been attempting to reverse-engineer it. Working under highly classified conditions, the PSD initiated Operation Zeitsprung. Teams of technicians were working around the clock to develop their own flying machine, or Wunderwaffe, powered by the captured alien; *'Electro-Temporal-Graviton'* engine, or the ETG engine as it became known. The scientists had discovered that the alien mechanism used infinite amounts of energy derived from a power source previously uncovered by the "Black Sun" project. It harnessed the energy from an invisible eternal light not visible to the human eye but existing in anti-matter. The energy output generated phenomenal power levels. A single engine was enough to power several cities.

Out of the thousands of individual components, one of the items removed from the original crashed disc was believed to be part of its navigation array and capable of guiding the craft across interstellar distances, using the Black-Sun power to create a time-shift. To look at it was a simple construction. A rectangular shaped box, roughly the same size as a Monopoly board with a grey metallic base, glass sides and a milk-white opaque surface. Yet, despite all the PSD technicians assigned to discovering the secrets of the box, it continued to elude their best efforts. Simply put, they could not get the device to work. It was categorised, labelled and sent to storage in the castle basement. No one noticed when two weeks ago, the box went missing.

"Herr General, look!" Professor von Riker called out. Glock looked at von Riker to see his face fixated on the box. He followed the Professors gaze to see what had caused his alarm. The planchette had begun moving around the surface by itself.

"This is truly remarkable!" von Riker exclaimed, "The box has learnt to operate autonomously. Before it needed two operators at either end to open the link and channel the spirit energy. Now it's as if...." He trailed off in thought.

"It thinks it's a telex machine?" Schaffer unhelpfully suggested.

Herr Stöller joined the triumvirate of Nazis. They all crowded closer to make out the message as it was repeatedly spelled out, one letter at a time.

"HEY FRITZ. LOOK AT MAJOR SCHAFFER."

All three looked up at where Major Schaffer was sitting. Glock regarded Schaffer with his usual impassive stare. Schaffer thought he detected a trace of emotion on the General's haggard face. Of course, he was mistaken.

"So, it was you all along. I always suspected that our agent in the future was you, Sturmbannführer Schaffer." Glock sneered.

"Not quite General. Consider me a double agent. The real agent is interrogating our subject about now, or discovering the cost of meddling with the natural progression of time." He allowed himself a small chuckle. "Only time will tell. However, future, past or present, I cannot allow you to continue. You must leave the boy alone."

Glock gave an intense stare as he meticulously pondered the meaning of Schaffer's comment. With dawning realisation his thin mouth formed a sinister smile.

"Such dedication to a future boy you have never met, Major. Why is that I wonder? Ach, but of course. I think I'm beginning to understand the way time travel works. Heinrich became a father. Or is it Heinrich becomes a father? These are semantics. Such a pity that young Herr Schaffer junior is going to become an orphan before he's even born." Glock reached for the holster on his hip.

A split second later a loud crack filled the room as the sharp report of Schaffer's Walther echoed around the low-ceilinged chamber.

All the while Glock had been talking, he hadn't seen Schaffer withdraw his pistol and train it on him from beneath the table. A jagged round hole appeared in the centre of the table, sending splinters of wood through the air along with the 9mm slug, straight at Glock's head. The General staggered backwards, his hand grasping at the bloody wound Schaffer's bullet had just made as it ripped through the flesh of his scraggy neck. With a disgusting gurgling, Glock collapsed to the ground, clawing his throat and choking on the ebbing pulses of his own blood as it spurted through his fingers. Sticky white spittle stretched between his lips as he mouthed something, but all he managed to produce was a ghostly sigh as the last of his breath ebbed away. Glock died with an unfinished sentence on his lips and his eyes wide open. A clawed hand frozen in a death rictus reached out and extended a single gnarled finger, pointing directly at Schaffer. Defying every convention of how a dead man remains dead, Glock's body simply vanished into thin air, leaving the acrid stench of cordite to fill the nostrils of the remaining men.

Stöller joined von Riker as they both watched in horror at a thin spiral of smoke, gently curling up from the pistol's muzzle. The Professor flinched as Schaffer trained the tip of his service weapon on him.

"Hands up, Gentlemen." Schaffer ordered at the two men.

Both men backed away, holding out their hands in a mixed gesture of surrender and pleading. The exit was barred by the portly figure of Sergeant Krupps, who had Lanz in a choke hold. Stöller and von Riker were just in time to see the life drain from the Gestapo man's eyes, as Krupps snapped his neck and let his lifeless body drop to the floor.

"Major, have you lost your mind?" von Riker stammered.

"Nein, Herr Professor." Schaffer replied. "On the contrary, I have blinked my eyes and cured my brain. I recognise evil when I am in its company. I am a proud German. I am not an animal. I must do what is necessary to prevent the misguided actions of lunatics like yourselves from destroying the world."

"And what about your murderous sergeant? Does he share your newly acquired departure of sanity?" This question came from Stöller.

"I doubt it." Schaffer replied, "But Krupps here is very loyal and will do almost anything for the promise of a cream filled bun."

Krupps reached into his pocket, retrieving one of the pastries he had swiped from the table. In one movement, the sergeant devoured the entire bun, before letting out a loud and sustained belch.

"Tut tut. Now then, mein kleiner Schweinefleisch. We may be in the company of 'Pigs' Sergeant." Schaffer spat the word. "But we must not forget our manners."

"You are both mad if you think you will get away with this!" Stöller exclaimed.

"The beauty of time travel, Herr Stöller, means we have already got away with it."

Stöller reached into the inside of his jacket, but the 9mm parabellum round from Schaffer's Walther caught him in the shoulder and spun him around with a violence that threw him to the ground. Stöller screamed in agony and clutched at his mangled shoulder. The pistol he was reaching for clattered to the floor and skidded across the wet stone flags, coming to a rest by the scientific equipment rack.

"Please." He pleaded through gritted teeth. "Mercy. I promise I won't say anything if you let me live." He scrambled across the floor, using his remaining good arm for support until his back was pressed up against the wall and he could go no further. He struggled to a standing position, his wounded shoulder causing him to adopt a slight hunch.

"That is what they always say, is it not Herr Stöller of the Gestapo?" Major Schaffer replied coolly, as he closed the gap on the cornered Nazi. "Oh, and for your information. My real name is not Schaffer. It is Meyer. Heinrich Meyer, son of Joseph David Meyer. My family lived in Lobeck Street. You should recognise that name."

Stöller lowered his eyes away from Schaffer's piercing gaze as he suddenly realised what the Major was talking about. Then, with a final show of indignance, Stöller spat at Heinrich.

"Meyer? Now I recognise that name. The pig Jew family from Berlin. The Kreuzberg district if I remember correctly?"

"And I remember it was you in charge of the operation. When your SA thugs were ordered to round us all up and throw us into cattle crates." Schaffer said, his eyes starting to water.

"You are nothing but filthy, stinking Juden. Your disgusting family got what they deserved. You though, you are a very clever Jew. To change your name and hide among the lions, typical Jewish trickery, your deceitful ways prove that we were right to drive your rotten race out of the Fatherland."

"Except my family wasn't driven out of the Fatherland, were they Herr Stöller? No, instead they were driven to Treblinka, where a deluded scientist called von Riker, performed unnatural experiments on my brother."

Von Riker bent down and scooped up the fallen pistol. "This is treason!" von Riker managed to say. Before he had a chance to aim the weapon, von Riker's eyes widened as the involuntary spasm of the optic muscle forced them to look upward, at a star-shaped hole splattered in the middle of his forehead. The force of the first bullet, burst out through the back of his head, dragging bits of skull and hair with it. His corpse hung in a gravity-defying suspension for a few seconds, then his eyes rolled upwards into the tops of their sockets. The pressure wave of Schaffer's second bullet ejected a gruesome gout of blood and brain matter, which was sucked out and splattered across the wall, like the brushstrokes of an angry child. The scientist's body was dead before it crashed into the array of instruments so carefully calibrated less than an hour ago and slumped into a heap. A blue tongue lolled out from the corner of his mouth and dribbled a stream of blood and saliva onto the crisp white lab coat.

"You are quite mad!" Stöller sobbed, regarding the fallen figure of the Professor at his feet. "Completely mad."

"Let me tell you what mad is, shall I. Mad is a twisted, paranoid commandant called Kurt Franz, who worked my father until he dropped dead of exhaustion." Schaffer squeezed the trigger again. The loud report of the pistol was deafening in the basement vault. Stöller winced and another grimace formed on his face.

"Mad is learning that your younger brother was gassed and his naked body left thrown on a heap." Another bullet found its mark. Tears were now streaming down both Schaffer's cheeks. "And you Herr Stöller, signed the warrant that sent my mother and sister to their deaths at Ravensbruck. That is the definition of MAD!"

The last squeeze of the trigger before Schaffer's pistol ran out of ammunition. Schaffer continued pointing the empty gun at his target. Only now there were just a series of clicks as the hammer struck the empty chamber. Stöller's body performed a macabre dance against the whitewashed wall as the bullets ripped into the cloth of his suit, plucking at the fabric in bursting fragments. Heinrich watched with grim satisfaction at the Gestapo man's heaving chest, as widening circles of blood welled up and soaked into his shirt. Dark rivulets dribbled down his trouser legs and dripped with wet splats onto his brogues. Stöller's wracked body slid down the wall leaving a large red smear that daubed the whitewash. Before the life-force completely departed his shattered body altogether, Stoller performed his last act of defiance and reached out a blood-soaked hand, pressing the alarm button. His corpse joined von Riker's on the floor. A limp hand flopped open and a small bloodstained piece of crumpled paper rolled out. Heinrich picked it up and inspected it. He saw a list of names scribbled next to dates, some in the past, others in the future. Each one had a brief order annotated next to it. Heinrich scanned down the list and stopped when he came to one of the entries.

'David Meyer. West Acton. London—2016. Son of Heinrich Meyer'

The order next to David's name brought a cold shiver to Heinrich.

'Capture-Interrogate-Eliminate. Recover Box B. Locate whereabouts of Heinrich Meyer, father of target subject. Discover real identity and execute. Suspect believed to be Sturmbannführer Schaffer.'

The penetrating klaxon of the alarm mixed with the sound of an alerted garrison of soldiers, rushing through the echoing corridors of the castle. The urgency of the situation intensified as the shouting grew louder. Major Schaffer's attention solidified and cemented his thinking to the current position. Which was not good. They were trapped in a room with no exit other than a single door, in which any moment a dozen armed guards would be pouring through.

"Krupps, quickly. Get the door." He barked.

Krupps hurried over to the double wooden doors of the chamber and heaved them shut. His podgy hands rammed the iron bolts into the holes. He grabbed up the heavy crossbeam and slid it into the brackets, sealing both himself and the Major in. The six-hundred-year-old wooden doors had been made from thick oak and were solid enough to keep even the most determined assailants at bay. As useful as Krupps had been, the Major knew they had only bought themselves a little time. Wood and stone would not hold up to a stick of Dynamite.

He scanned the interior of the chamber, looking for anything that would help. "Come on, there must be something, think. These weirdos are amongst the most paranoid people on the planet. They wouldn't deliberately place themselves in a room with no means of escape. They are all cowards."

A frantic clamouring of the doors announced that the soldiers had arrived. Schaffer could picture the scene playing out on the other side of the barricaded doors. The men would be trying to shoulder the doors open at first. Then one or two would kick at the doors, before realising how solid they were. They may attempt to form a battering party and rush at the door together. And then the duty officer will sweep in, late to the party but brimming with his usual arrogance. He will assess the situation and go straight for the quickest method. A soldier will be sent to the armoury to collect a stick of explosive and a detonator. He will return and place the charge on the door and the soldiers will retreat around the corner of the corridor, where the plunger will be initiated and the charge will detonate, reducing the door to matchwood. The first items to come through the door will be a couple of stick grenades, which with explode in five or seven seconds, sending red-hot splinters of metal ripping through the room. Then the soldiers will storm the room and shoot anyone still standing with their MP40 machine pistols.

"Which means we have approximately twelve minutes to find a way out." He absentmindedly announced to the room.

The initial battering coming from behind the doors had stopped and a calmness lulled the room. "That will be the order to retrieve the Dynamite." Schaffer noted. They both backed over to the grand inglenook fireplace and started to inspect it. Centuries of soot had marked the brickwork from the countless fires that had burned in the grate. Schaffer smacked the solid stone in frustration. "Bah! This is useless. Let's face it Krupps, the war is over for us my friend."

From the corridor they heard the muffled order to take cover. In a few seconds the door would be blown to smithereens.

Schaffer released the magazine from his pistol and looked at the empty clip. He threw the useless weapon away and straighten his uniform. If he was to die in a hail of bullets, at least he would be dressed respectably. Out of the corner of his eye, Schaffer noticed the box which was still sitting on top of the alter. He walked over to it and scooped it up, rejoining Krupps underneath the fireplace, he turned and regarded his friend.

"Sergeant Krupps, thank you for being my adjutant and my friend. Farewell, Gunther." Schaffer raised the box above his head.

Krupps grabbed the iron poker hanging from the fireplace, in a last-ditch attempt to fight with.

The door disintegrated in a fiery explosion, sending high velocity chunks of shattered wood and lethal splinters into the chamber. A second later, two sticks tumbled in through the smoke and clattered across the floor. They detonated in unison, five point five seconds later. The soldiers filed in, indiscriminately spraying the chamber with their MP40's. The bullets struck the remaining relics and artwork left intact after the explosions, smashing them to ruins.

"Cease fire." The duty officer commanded.

The breeching party peered through the clearing smoke, straining to verify that their assault was successful. Two bodies lay, half-buried under fallen wood and masonry. The soldiers fanned out and completed their sweep of the room before reporting back to the officer.

"The room is all clear, sir. Two dead. No survivors."

The officer accepted the report and turned on his heels. "Everyone out." He ordered.

The Hall of the Dead deserved its moniker. And now it had two more dead to its name.

—

"For once, time is on the side of the just." Heinrich breathed from behind the protective walls of the grand inglenook fireplace, as it swivelled shut moments before the door blew in.

"Krupps, if you hadn't found that secret switch, we'd both be eating buns in the sky by now."

Sergeant Krupps looked at the heavy iron poker in his hand. Not realising that the moment he'd lifted it up, a hidden mechanism disengaged and the sprung loaded turntable spun the entire fire grate, including its two hapless passengers, revealing a secret passage on the other side and their route to escape. The soldiers had seen the mangled, half-buried bodies of the professor and the gestapo man and incorrectly assumed that no one else had survived.

CHAPTER 11

(EPILOGUE)

LONDON—2016

Vossmeister finally ran out of goodwill. "Very well Herr Meyer, if you do not wish to come out and play, we will come to you." He nodded to the adjutant stood next to him. "Send in the troops."

The adjutant retrieved a whistle from his tunic pocket and brought it to his pursed lips. He drew a sharp intake of breath and was about to blow when Vossmeister stopped him.

"WAIT!" He barked. The adjutant faltered, dropping the whistle where it hung from its lanyard around his neck. Vossmeister smirked. "I have a better idea. Send in the Red Devils."

The adjutant visibly winced at Vossmeister's order. "Those things give me the creeps." He said, lifting a radio handset and depressing the button. "Mobilise Red Squadron."

A lone vehicle lumbered onto the street. It stopped with a hiss of escaping air from its brakes. The tail gate lowered to the ground on hydraulic rams. Moments later the steady march of boots descended the metallic ramp. A detachment of eight clone soldiers lined up at the kerbside in two rows. They wore tactical armoured SS uniforms with red swastika armbands. The tops of their heads were protected by black steel M40 helmets bearing the Nazi rune insignia and their faces were concealed by black respirators. They were equipped with the latest pulse rifles, armed with Black Sun rounds. An inexhaustible supply of ammunition, each with the destructive power of a cannon. A bright red glow emanated from behind the polycarbonate lenses of their masks.

"Squad." Vossmeister brought the soldiers to attention. "Advance." The squadron set off in unison with robotic precision, heading towards the house.

Inside, David was still held under the trance-like state of the box. He was oblivious to the advancing soldiers. Mrs Reynolds heard the splintering of wood as the front door gave way. She hurried to the top of the landing in time to see the first soldier mount the stairs.

"Hurry up, David." She cried, "They're coming. Whatever it is you're doing, do it faster."

The lead augmented soldier continued his advance, progressing up the stairs. The red glow from his eyes casting an eerie shadow on the walls. From behind her back, Mrs Reynolds produced a Webley MK VI service revolver and with a trembling hand pointed it at the soldier.

"Those two old men said all I had to do was point and click. Here goes. Stay back!" She shouted. The soldier continued his inexorable climb.

Mrs Reynolds drew back the hammer and the revolver's cylinder rotated once, aligning the .455 brass cartridge with the breech opening. As she squeezed the trigger the steel firing pin rammed home on the percussion cap, sending the initiating charge into the main cartridge casing, where it ignited the crystalised cordite within. A rapid build up of superheated gasses pushed the 17.2 gramme lead ball at 650 feet per second along the rifled grooves of the short barrel, expelling the projectile in a cloud of hot gas and smoke and sending it on a lethal trajectory towards the soldier. The bullet found it's mark and pierced the front of the steel helmet. The velocity carried the lead ball into the cranium of the soldier, instantly halting his advance. The soldier stumbled, falling forward before slumping back down the stairs. His position was immediately replaced by another clone. Mrs Reynolds continued to fire, issuing a fusillade of deadly lead into the air. The second soldier's body was punctured by two rounds, throwing him back down the stairs to join his fallen kamerad, still they came. A bloody tangle of bodies blocked the bottom of the stairs, as the inevitable happened and the dry click of the revolver signalled that Mrs Reynolds had run out of ammunition.

She watched in horror as the blood-soaked corpses started to stand up again, their bodies reanimated by an unholy force. The deformed bullets from Mrs Reynolds gun were pushed out of the soldier's bodies, where they clattered harmlessly to the floor. The ragged flesh around the dark entry holes knitted back together in front of her disbelieving eyes. With all trace of the wounds gone, the unnatural soldiers resumed their advance.

Gasping at the demonic sight in front of her, she turned to the bathroom door and stammered in shock. "DAVID…NOW!"

Her cries were severed at their source as the lead soldier arrived at the top of the stairs and grabbed her by the throat. He lifted her body into the air and squeezed with the might of a boa constrictor. Mrs Reynolds eyes bulged in their sockets. She clawed at his hand in desperation, choking, but his hold on her was iron-clad. Her larynx crushed and her lungs finally starved of oxygen she slumped; her body held limp in his outstretched arm. A thin drool of saliva trickled down his gloved hand. There was a metallic tinkling noise as a small round badge fell from her frock and rolled across the landing. It came to a spinning rest at David's feet. He picked it up and saw the black arms of the swastika surrounded by the words... 'Meine Ehre heißt Treue'.

David's senses came rushing back to him as he shook his head to clear away the last traces of the spell. He snatched up the box and stepped onto the landing in time to see Mrs Reynolds being cast aside. He watched as she landed in a crumpled heap, like a ball of dirty laundry. Twice now, Mrs Reynolds had died in his time.

He sprinted into his room and locked the door a fraction before the soldier reached the handle and began to wrench it. The flimsy lock put up no resistance to the superhuman grip of the red eyed soldier and the door burst open. David backed towards his window, but he knew escape was impossible. He had to destroy the box. He spun on his heels, letting the box slip from his hands and hurled it as hard as he could. The soldier reached him a split-second later, the demonic red eyes burning behind the mask, like Hell's inferno. With one swipe he delivered a crippling blow to his kidneys. David shrieked in agony and collapsed onto the floor. The soldier's boot was suspended in the air, hovering above David's head. David screwed his eyes shut and waited for the crushing blow of the soldier's boot to come crashing down onto his head. Nothing happened.

The box crashed through the plate glass window and sailed through the air, spinning in a prescribed arc. Following its trajectory were the keen eyes of a soldier posted to the rear of the property. The box continued its flight towards his outstretched arms and was certain to land in them, as safely as a well caught football, but for a momentary distraction coming from the rear service road. The soldier was struck on the side of the face by a stale pastry. The concealed assailant only revealing his position by saying. "POW! Right in the kisser."

The box brushed the stunned soldier's fingertips and skimmed over his head, caroming off his steel helmet. With explosive force it crashed into the garden wall and shattered against the brickwork. The Red Eyed Devil, with his boot poised to deliver the killer blow to David's head, had frozen in time for a fraction of a second, before dissolving into a blanket of acrid ash.

In the same instant the goalkeeping soldier's body also began to contort, as it was wracked with crippling spasms. His mouth froze into the twisted rictus of a battlefield death grimace. The skin on his face turned ash-grey and dissolved, peeling back from his forehead, revealing the bleach-white bone of his skull. He sagged down onto the grass, his body convulsing as a pure black energy wave erupted from every orifice of his head. Like a violent torrent of flies vomiting from his mouth, the energy wave connected to every soldier in turn. David managed to crawl to the window and hauled himself up in time to watch as the soldiers lining the street succumbed to the contagion, liquifying as the black wave jumped from one to the other, consuming their bodies. The sky crackled with an angry buzzing.

"Yuck…Gross! And that is why you shouldn't go around with your mouth open." David shouted.

The impact severed the boxes temporal link, sending a high energy feedback wave coursing back along the timeline. Anything and anyone existing from the concept of the NAZI established timeline, was instantaneously destroyed. At exactly 22:01, the containment field failed and a nanosecond after that, the fractured antimatter chamber mixed the Black Sun energy with normal matter and the heart of the box erupted in a blinding white flash. With the explosive force of a hundred nuclear detonations, the blast wave enveloped the surrounding area, annihilating everything in its path. The leading edge of the pulsating energy wave expanded at faster-than-light speed, engulfing the entire Capital.

The soldiers had gone, vanished in the blink of an eye. Gone too was the occupied vista of London. But there was no trail of death or destruction left behind in the explosion's wake. Instead stood a modern city complete with red brick houses and streets lined with people going about their normal everyday business. The London Eye rotated its sightseeing passengers in a lazy arc. Big Ben chimed the hour as below it, ministers argued policies in Parliament. Worshipers flocked to the domed St Pauls cathedral, designed and built by Sir Christopher Wren.

There was a creaking noise from the floorboard outside David's room. He snatched open the door to reveal a fully restored Mrs Reynolds, with a look of surprise mixed with suspicion on her face. Another figure was loitering further down the landing. Mrs Reynolds turned and snapped at the man with a shrill tongue.

"Haven't you got to take the bins out, Bert? And don't forget the washing machine needs fixing. You still need to cut the hedge."

The man retrieved a half-smoked stogie from behind his ear and sauntered off with a copy of the Racing Post underneath his arm. "Alright, alright already. Don't get your gusset in a bind, Doris. If I could use your tongue, I'll have the hedge done in no time."

"And don't think that you can hide in your shed listening to the racing on that radio either, Bert Reynolds." Her husband suitably chastised, she returned her attentions to David.

"Rent!" She blurted out, accompanied by a pudgy, outstretched hand.

"Nazis." David instinctively replied.

He flew past his flabbergasted landlady and down the stairs, passing Mr Reynolds on the way.

"She missed you when you were dead, Mr R." He said, before bounding out of the front door.

"I imagine it was very peaceful, my boy?" Mr Reynolds muttered as he headed to his shed.

David made straight for the high street. He paused at the antique shop to discover a 'To Let' board hanging outside. The doors and windows were boarded up and decade's worth of graffiti daubed the building. Two elderly gentlemen approached him from across the road.

"Excuse me." David hailed to the taller of the two men. "What happened to this shop?" He asked.

"That old place has been derelict for years." The old man said. "After an unexplained explosion."

"Explosion!?" David exclaimed. "I don't remember any explosion."

"If you ask me, they ought to knock it down." This came from the tubby man eating a cold strudel. "And build a cake shop in its place. Care for a pastry, mein freund." He offered up a crumpled paper bag to David. David politely declined.

"That's enough, Gunther. Not everybody has the same insatiable appetite as you for confectionary." The tall mad said.

"Please excuse my fat friend. Forgive my intrusion, but that is a nice-looking watch you have there. Does it tell the right time?"

David looked at the man, then at his watch before answering. "Nah. Sorry…it's never worked. I don't know why I wear it to be honest. I just like it I guess."

"Would you mind?" The man asked, as he grabbed David's wrist and lifted it up to examine it without waiting for permission. "Ahh, this is a German timepiece. Made in Dusseldorf. Quite rare, but also quite worthless I'm afraid." He placed his hands over the watch and pressed firmly before letting go of David's wrist, which flopped back to his side.

David shrugged and gave a half-smile. "That's about right for me." He said in a conciliatory tone.

"Please, take this. I insist." Before David could resist, Gunther squashed a sticky pastry into his pocket. "You never know when you may need it."

"Thanks." David left the two men standing outside the derelict shop and hurried away.

"Goodbye mien Son." The old man said, wiping a tear away after David was gone. The two elderly men walked off, their bodies fading into the Universe.

The last loose ends of time were repairing themselves. Final adjustments were being made at a Cosmological level.

David continued along the street until he reached the bank and fumbled for his card. He thrust it into the slot and stabbed in his PIN code with such force, he thought his fingers would snap. The machine whirred, oblivious to the urgency its customer was demanding. After what seemed like an eternity in time to David, the ATM beeped its customary beep and displayed the information he had requested.

'Your Account Balance is. . . OVERDRAWN BY - £78. Your Card Has Been Retained'

David looked at his watch. 22:02...and counting.

"Get in." He shouted to the world.

Printed in Great Britain
by Amazon